Amalie Berlin lives with her family and her critters in Southern Ohio, and writes quirky and independent characters for Mills & Boon Medical Romance. She likes to buck expectations with unusual settings and situations, and believes humour can be used powerfully to illuminate the truth—especially when juxtaposed against intense emotions. Love is stronger and more satisfying when your partner can make you laugh through the times when you don't have the luxury of tears.

HEALED UNDER THE MISTLETOE

AMALIE BERLIN

MILLS & BOON

First Published in Great Britain 2018
by Mills & Boon, an imprint of HarperCollins*Publishers*
1 London Bridge Street, London, SE1 9GF

© 2018 Amalie Berlin

ISBN: 978-0-263-93387-1

MIX
Paper from
responsible sources
FSC C007454

This book is produced from independently certified FSC™ paper
to ensure responsible forest management.
For more information visit www.harpercollins.co.uk/green.

Printed and bound in Spain
by CPI, Barcelona

Dedicated to my brother, Seth,
and all the stories he has left to tell.

CHAPTER ONE

NURSE PRACTITIONER YSABELLE SABETTA signed the last page of her employment paperwork and slid the bundle back across the desk.

No matter how many times she did it, her first day in a new facility always filled Belle with a mix of excitement and anxiety. She did it a lot, in fact, since she had only worked in contracted, short-term positions since she'd been accredited, first at home in Arizona, and then in neighboring southwestern states. This time the process was different: she'd taken the position straight out, and still wasn't sure why she'd done that. Once the signings were complete, she'd be a full-time employee of a Manhattan hospital.

Her sister would've approved of this move, living in New York, a city they'd always felt linked to by their grandmother, who'd been born and raised in Queens, but followed to Arizona the injured soldier she'd fallen for while tending him in Korea during the war.

After a lifetime of Nanna's stories about magical New York Christmases, the girls had vowed to make it there for the Christmas season so many times, but Belle had only made it after Noelle died.

She was never supposed to be there alone. But she was. She'd been there three days and although she was able to keep clear-headed most of the time, sometimes the world around her seemed to have sped up or she'd slowed down, as if she was out of pace with not only the city, but reality. The world didn't spin, but the sensation was there deep in her chest, as if her inner gyroscope were broken and everything around her were spinning.

Nothing good could come from dwelling on it right now. Not on her first day. Really not on her first day in the biggest city she'd ever visited, let alone moved to—a place that might be too big for her, too much for her.

She had no idea what she might encounter, aside from the sort of situations depicted in horror-story documentaries about life in the ER, and sexy television medical dramas. Which narrowed expectations down to removing some bizarre item from a place it should've never been stuck, and a sexy rendezvous in the supply room with an arrogant ladies' man who saved lives in between supply-room romps.

Or maybe she'd be taken hostage by an injured criminal who somehow had gotten a disposed syringe from the sharps container, filled with a mysterious cleaning fluid, and stabbed her in the neck while threatening to fill her carotid with something caustic and deadly if they didn't give him a helicopter and a million dollars in untraceable bills. Anything was possible.

What curdled this morning's coffee was more terror-tinged anxiety than excitement, mixed with the nitroglycerin-like certainty that she'd made a terrible mistake. That New York was too big for her, even outside work. She'd always been the timid twin—Noelle could stare down a dragon and Belle had once been cowed by a grumpy chihuahua.

"I hope you'll enjoy your time at Sutcliffe Memorial, Ms. Sabetta." The woman handling her paperwork smiled, showing no teeth and no warmth. A smile with too much knowing in it to inspire confidence, as if she could read anxiety in Belle's penmanship.

She peered at her signature, half convinced she'd see the same shakiness that had seeped into Nanna's penmanship near the end.

Once again, Ms. Masterson went over the guidelines of the probationary period, delineating the date where she'd become officially an employee of Sutcliffe, and the restrictions. Belle initialed where appropriate, and kept up the polite conversation expected of her. "I'll look forward to that date and…"

Muffled alarm bounced off the closed office door, stalling her words and kicking her pulse up a notch.

Raised voices.

A woman's voice. Maybe the assistant who'd seen her in earlier. What had she said?

She twisted to look at the door, muscles tense, ready to run one way or another, then turned again to Masterson. It was her office. If she should be alarmed by the commotion, as the prickling sensation on the back of Belle's neck argued, Masterson would show it.

People shouted in hospitals more than one would think. People in pain couldn't be faulted, but that wasn't the only reason people lost control. Emotions ran high where life-and-death decisions happened. People got angry. Sometimes people were delusional and not capable of controlling outbursts. Sometimes, even more sadly, outbursts were prompted by mind-altering substances.

But this office was nowhere near treatment facilities. It was an office at the end of a hallway packed with other offices.

Masterson's calm, slow head tilt didn't clarify whether Belle's alarm was unfounded, but the shift of her gaze over Belle's shoulder to the door behind her said enough. Paying extra attention to a commotion? A distinct reason for alarm.

Unable to help herself, as the voices continued—now with a deep, clipped masculine voice breaking through—Belle twisted back to watch the door in case a madman burst in.

"Should we check?"

The sudden swing of the door, combined with that hyperalert prickling of her skin, launched her from the chair. She whirled to face the coming danger, every muscle balled and ready to do…something.

A tall, broad-shouldered man in scrubs strode in, a sheet of *paper* held in one hand—not a weapon. He glanced at her, but she clearly wasn't who he'd come to see, as his glacial blue eyes returned to Masterson, still in her chair, far more at ease than Belle.

Past him, she could see the assistant hovering in the doorway, looking apologetic and worried.

"I'm not doing it," the man said without preamble, giving the paper a flick to send it fluttering onto Masterson's desk. "I've told you twice, I'll not be dragged into this holiday madness. I'm not my brother—he can be Administration's puppet."

He had an accent, there but slight, and the man projected such unpleasantness, she didn't want the little thrill his accent stirred. Didn't want to examine it.

It reminded her of a person who'd spent their first ten years in another country but moved early enough to nearly lose their original accent. However, the clipped, perfectly enunciated words were like another language entirely; fluent irritation was the strongest accent she heard, strong enough it was impossible to miss.

"Your brother isn't a puppet, Dr. McKeag," Masterson said, reaching for the paper to read it.

The fact that Belle had leaped from her seat as one might a burning building went blessedly unacknowledged, but that did nothing to diminish the creeping sense of foolishness inching down her spine. Still standing out of the way of an irritated, paper-wielding doctor? All remnants of her nurse's pride bristled.

He was just so close to her chair. Returning to it felt like sitting on a snake's rattler but moving farther away would look as if she was every bit as intimidated as she felt, especially when he looked at her and those ice-shard eyes shouted at her.

I see you.

I know I'm interrupting.

I don't give a damn.

It wasn't that he reeked anger, but she couldn't imagine anyone missing the cold, disdainful irritation that put him above, somehow. It was almost how she'd picture an angry king, forced to communicate with his lowly, and possibly scabby, subjects. Superior. Arrogant. *Bothered.*

If the universe had any affection for her, this would be her only interaction with him. Ever. Even if she was intrigued by the accent. And his shoulders.

"Isn't Wolfe doing enough of this nonsense with Conley? I suppose it's somewhat suiting to Pediatrics, but it's beneath the other departments. This is Manhattan, not the North Pole Hospital."

"I'm sure your inclusion was a mistake, Dr. McKeag," Masterson said, looking a little bit bored. "And there's no need to be sarcastic."

Hands free of the offending paper, now propped onto his narrow hips, drawing her attention again to the breadth of his shoulders. The black scrubs stretched tight across his chest, defining everything. Impressive torso: one more shallow mark in his favor. Also, as inappropriate of her to dwell on as the man's other attributes. Like his haircut: a strange mix of a carelessly natural, longish top and neckline razored to perfection. His hair should not matter.

"I'm a Scot. It's genetic." He said this so precisely she wanted to believe him. She could see the title of the imaginary medical journal article now: *Sarcasm Gene Discovered in Ancient Scottish Burial Site.*

The deadpan way he delivered it said he wasn't done, no wrap-this-up inflection to his words, even though he'd just won. Masterson's words were both admission and apology. The argument should be over. He should be *going.* Belle would like to get back to the business of finishing her paperwork, so she could get to the Emergency Department and get on with being out of her depth and out of her mind to take this position in the first place.

"Good." He looked at her again and the curiosity she didn't want to feel bloomed into life, a sign Belle should sit back down so he would be out of her line of sight and less inclined to sexually harass him in her mind—something he'd surely see on her face if he had any intuition or experience with women, which he certainly did, looking like that.

He wasn't her type anyway, even if his attractiveness could counter his personality. Belle tended to date the kind of man who never stormed anywhere, outside video games. And, generally, only had the broad-shoulder thing happening in the avatars they selected. They were kind, quiet, intelligent and *introverted*, like her. Storming anywhere besides a digital castle to fight an electronic troll would never, ever occur to them.

The mental comparison conjured him in a set of armor, a battered iron helmet, with a broadsword, and was somehow less laughable than she would've hoped. Instead, it made her think of the sexy Viking book she'd read the other day.

Whatever. She was going to sit. Not stand there and stare at the man.

Pretend he wasn't standing close to the chair she was foolish to continue avoiding when he wasn't a threat, just exceedingly cranky about a Christmas molehill. Irritating. Not dangerous. She'd moved to New York City and had to act like it. Have some gumption. Decide he could just take his impressive torso, enviably square jaw, and step to the side to avoid standing close to *her*.

Yeah! Lie to herself. Might as well. Vigorous denial got her through everything else in her life, let her pretend she wasn't the last Sabetta standing.

She sighed before she could stop herself, but Masterson's glance pushed those thoughts aside.

She was usually better at putting away the misery she'd been avoiding for over a year, but since she'd arrived in New York her subconscious had waged a near constant assault.

She took a breath, stepped right back to the chair and sat, keeping him and his dark, foreboding shoulders out of view.

But not far enough away that she couldn't still feel him, looming like a thundercloud in his black scrubs.

She glanced down into the bag still sitting beside her chair where she'd stashed the three sets of departmental scrubs she'd been provided. *The black scrubs.*

Her stomach dropped.

Damn. He was from Emergency, and this rude showdown wasn't even related to the job. Nothing to do with patient care. She liked to think of all medical professionals having the guts to go to the mat for their patients, but all this was about Christmas activities?

One glance over her shoulder confirmed the sharp set of his clean-shaven jaw was not that of a happy man. The dissonance between his reaction to the event and the importance of it clanged like a gong in her ear.

If anyone understood dreading the holidays, it was her. Thanksgiving had been bad enough the past couple of years, but Christmas was worse.

Although her family had a history of service—starting with Nanna exchanging her white cap for fatigues to serve in the Korean War, continuing with Dad, a Scottsdale policeman until his death, to Belle becoming a nurse—Noelle had started her career as a flight attendant, then secured flight training and become one of the few female pilots in a major commercial airline. Her life had been flying around the world, gone most of the time, but she'd always come back home for Christmas. At least for long enough to fetch Belle for their traditional adventure.

They were *always* together for Christmas, and that now made the season about two months of misery.

Yet, even she—with her impossibly good reasons to

dread the season—couldn't drum up this level of irritation at being *included* by someone.

The muscle at the corner of his ridiculously square jaw bunched and flexed, bunched and flexed, and could be doing nothing but gritting and grinding his back teeth. Not irritated. *Angry.*

"Emergency, of all departments, is too busy and too critical for this kind of nonsense to take up space in anyone's head. Lives are on the line."

This was him holding back? Boggled the mind.

"This is a hospital. Lives are on the line in all departments."

"And in Emergency, the line is much narrower than most other departments. It's the *front line*. People need to be focused, not distracted by and gossiping about orchestrated, compulsory…festivities."

The pause that lingered before he uttered the word *festivities* spoke to this civilized visage he projected to cover some of his anger, but her mind supplied several less civilized words that better expressed his vibe, and Nanna's mantra sprang to mind right behind it: *People who hurt others are suffering too. Suffering.*

No. Nope. Not thinking that today either. She didn't have space left in her head to worry about a random, cranky doctor on her first day in a job that was probably too big for her anyway.

"It's just a holiday gift exchange."

"And it can occur without my participation, as can anything else that's being planned. I hope the third time is the charm, as I've made this request twice, then found that slid into my locker this morning."

If anyone *needed* Christmas…

"There's nothing else planned as yet for Emergency." Masterson smiled again, but the corners of her mouth barely lifted. It might not even be a smile, maybe it was an extremely pleasant grimace. Unpleasant smile, highly pleasant grimace.

Sliding the offending invitation out of the way, Masterson moved on with a gesture to Belle, where she sat with McKeag still over her shoulder.

"This is Ysabelle Sabetta, your new nurse practitioner." And there went her stomach again. Nervous to get going, or hating being the focus of attention. Or dreading being labeled *his*. Dread. That was totally dread.

"I was about to call down to get Dr. Backeljauw to send for her. We've agreed she's to shadow you today, learn the ropes before she's assigned her own patients." By the time Masterson had gotten it out, Belle's soul had sunk right through her body and seeped out of her toes, which was probably why it took so much effort to stand back up, but she had to stand. It was either that or implode like a socially awkward black hole and wink out of existence.

She stuck her hand out, mustered a smile and waited.

Although he looked at her hand, his attention shot back to Masterson. "I'll take her down, but I don't need a nurse practitioner."

Rejected.

She let her hand fall, but he caught it before she got away.

His hand was large and warm and drew attention to how cold her hands always were, now enfolded in his warmth. Another mark in the pleasant column for this unpleasant man. He didn't shake right away. When she met his gaze, the coldness she'd seen in his pale blue eyes had dimmed a bit. Only a little and only for a second—so fleeting she couldn't be sure she hadn't imagined it—but it reappeared after the obligatory shake and withdrawal.

"Have you just received your license?" The first time he'd spoken directly to her, and that was what he said? Maybe he *didn't* have experience with women, even looking as if he did.

She didn't flinch, although it took a second for her to decide how to take his words.

Kindly, she decided, with the benefit of the doubt that he didn't mean to be rude, despite all she'd seen of him so far. Rude people, mean people, insufferable and just plain unpleasant people were the ones who needed kindness the most. They needed the greatest benefit of the doubt.

The *kind* interpretation: his question was about how old she looked. She *did* look younger than her years and had heard so with annoying frequency since she actually was young.

Normally, it didn't bother her, but on the heels of everything that had gone on this morning—coupled with his tone—it took effort to take it kindly, and not as an insinuation she wasn't up to the task.

Which rankled.

Even if she *might not* be up to the task and had been questioning that too since before he'd barged in.

"Three years ago." Words. An answer. Truthful, and not even said with the frustration making her forehead tight.

"Three years," he repeated, turning to Masterson. "She doesn't need to shadow anyone. I'll bring her down, but she's not a child. She doesn't need babysitting."

Another whiplash turn. Insults to expressions of faith? Or just getting out of spending more time with her specifically, for whatever reason.

The idea of being lassoed to him for a day sounded about as appealing as a root canal, but she'd rather admit to possible inadequacy than risk patient lives, and they'd picked him for a reason—probably *not* because he was a bad doctor.

"I usually work in small facilities—Urgent Cares and small-town emergency rooms, which send their critical patients to bigger cities with trauma wards, usually before they get to the hospital. I haven't seen much, if any, intense, man-made trauma. Although I appreciate the vote of confidence, I haven't earned it."

But she hoped to sort out the position and her capability before three months were up. The earlier the better, so if she needed to run, she could just go, no harm, no foul. They could fire her without much explanation in that time too, but she should be able to judge her inadequacy first, regardless of whoever got stuck *babysitting* her.

It didn't need to be him.

It was still an insulting word, but she'd take whoever would allow her to shadow them.

"Take it up with Backeljauw," Masterson said, stepping neatly out of the discussion and standing up. "Good luck, Ms. Sabetta. Welcome again. Don't let McKeag scare you off—he's not the brother we use for PR for a reason."

McKeag gave a long-suffering eye-roll, looked at her clothes, then turned. "Come on. We'll go to the locker room, you can quickly change, and we'll continue to Emergency."

CHAPTER TWO

LYONS STRODE OUT of Masterson's office, his spine nearly creaking from the tightness that had seized every muscle in his body since he'd found that ridiculous Christmas assignment.

Despite the carpet inside the office of Human Resources, he could make out the sound of movement behind him. Either she was following, or the ever-flailing assistant was. He didn't pause to check; she'd follow now or someone else would escort her down later.

He couldn't afford to coddle the woman. If he could exchange his family's fortune for time, he would. When he was on duty, there was never enough of it. There hadn't been enough for his trip to HR this morning, but he'd gone anyway, intending it to be short. But it had already been too long. Who knew what had come into Emergency in his absence? If he wasn't there, he couldn't keep an eye out for inevitable trouble.

No matter how called he felt to emergency medicine, Lyons knew from hard experience the sorts of people who came in. Pediatric specialists might treat innocent children, but were exposed to their unsavory parents too, or had to treat the aftermath of abuse. Those who practiced widely, engaging in everyday emergency medicine, could see kindly grandmothers or men who'd injured themselves while beating another person to death. Patients with police escorts, cuffed because they were a danger to others, not that it always did much good. Trauma surgeons often treated the already unconscious, but afterward had to deal with those who'd accompanied the patient—people who might turn violent when given bad news.

Or worse, in the high flow of traffic in and out of Emergency, a madman with a gun could blend in and just start shooting. That happened here.

He hit the hallway without breaking stride. On a good day, he didn't have time to coddle the woman, and that was without Christmas insanity being added into the mix.

His main task was vigilance, and medicine came second. He had to do what he'd failed to do last Christmas and pay attention to what his gut had been saying then and was saying now.

He heard rapid footfalls on the hallway's tiled floors behind him—two steps for every one of his to catch up—and called over his shoulder, "Quickly."

The difference between this Christmas and last Christmas was him understanding what his gut was saying. The three bullets fired into him by the husband of a colleague had become his gut's Rosetta stone, the wake-up call that made him pay attention to everything—both for his own benefit and those who hadn't had the misfortune to share in his life lessons.

Even without the sound of her scurrying, her presence heated his back. For once, that awareness of someone behind him didn't prickle like danger. He just *felt* her there. Awareness that bothered by its nature, by the way it fractured his attention. She might not be a physical danger, but the way he heard and categorized her sounds—breath, step, fidget—was by robbing his concentration.

It was out of character for him to feel anything, really, except for the tension he'd become so intimate with he even carried it into his sleep. Mistrust of everyone, including himself, was also a constant companion. The attraction sparked by this woman—because he wouldn't lie to himself; that was what it was—he didn't like. Didn't want.

Still, he had to be civil. This was his workplace; he only yelled when someone deserved it. Just get this done quickly, hand her off to Backeljauw for reassignment and get back on duty.

Breaking his habit, he stopped at the lift and summoned it, giving her a chance to catch up.

She stepped into his side vision, beckoning him to look at her fully again, for the flaws that had to be there. He was usually good at finding the unpleasant aspects of other people; they would take some shine off.

His first thought upon having seen her, standing across the office from him, her eyes wild and obviously frightened, had been predatory but restrained. The door hadn't slammed. He hadn't raised his voice, not once, but she'd still looked at him as if he'd been a barely leashed bear about to eat her up.

The thought, the sexual grind of it—sudden and unexpected—made his lower abdomen contract and start to heat.

Damn. Look harder, find the flaw.

He scanned her features. "Are you ready for this?"

The grim set of her soft mouth said no, but that wasn't the flaw.

"Yes."

Her lie was a flaw, but not in her appearance. Still not helping.

Neither was her silky, brilliantly colored hair. Sorrel, it was like sorrel.

Still not the flaw—even if it prompted him to think of her in equine descriptors. Disturbing, but his flaw if it was one, that and a dearth of words to name that rich color. Earthy brown with fire and gold mingled in. Not her flaw.

The braided knot she wore it in suggested length and would've looked very professional but for the curling lock in the front that bounced free no matter how frequently she tucked it behind her ear. She looked more as if she should be selling some upscale shampoo than wearing scrubs. Which she wasn't wearing yet.

"Locker room first," he muttered, trying to put himself back on track, then continued picturing horses because it seemed like the thing to do. A way to keep himself from dwelling on the fact he was taking her somewhere to take her clothes off and change into the scrubs she'd been given. He shouldn't be thinking like that. She was practically a child.

That was the flaw. The thing he could cling to: common damned decency. She was too young. That would keep his unexpected flare of interest under control.

He locked his gaze to her nearly black eyes. "Did you work at all as a nurse before pursuing your advanced license?"

Her brows came together, forming the only line he could see on her face, and taking away a little bit of that wide-eyed vulnerability he kept seeing when he looked at her.

"I worked as an RN for three years before returning to school for another two years."

"And you were licensed three years ago." He remembered that as well. Laws existed to keep him from asking her age, but he could ask questions about her experience and qualifications, which would let him estimate.

Eight years ago she became an RN. It would've taken at least two, but more likely four, years to have become an RN. Likely twelve years of combined work experience and education. She was certainly no younger than twenty-eight, but probably closer to thirty.

Didn't look it, but it was still enough of a gap for him to work with. Coupled with his track record with not getting involved on any personal level with colleagues at Christmastime helped solidify his determination. That and duty.

He might not know when the danger his gut warned against would arrive, but he knew it would come.

The elevator finally dinged, and he stepped in with her right behind him. Both of them remained silent for the rest of the journey. All he heard outside the hospital's PA system, and the lullaby music that played announcing a birth in the hospital, were her rapid footfalls to keep up with him in the hallway once they reached their floor, and the plummeting of his own thoughts.

"Locker room," he finally stated, pushing in. "What locker were you assigned?"

She gave the number, two down from his own locker, naturally, and he led her around the middle bank of lockers to locate it. She pulled a small envelope from her pocket with the locker number written on it. Key. Good.

Time to hurry this up.

"Two minutes." He checked his watch, then gestured to the locker. "Get changed, come out to the hall. Two minutes." All the time he was willing to spare for babysitting.

He exited the way they'd come, back to where he wouldn't be tempted to peek at her undressing—despite the self-disgust that came with it, he knew it'd be a struggle to contain the desire to look as he heard her peeling off that creamy blouse and black trousers.

Safely outside, he leaned and shifted his attention from picturing horses, in an attempt to control his thoughts, to the cases he'd left being seen in Emergency. Specifically, the man who vibrated with ill intentions and who'd given Lyons something more than paranoid ideas, gave him genuine cause for concern.

Was she done? How long could it take to change?

It had been so long since he'd felt a tiny spark of desire, he didn't quite know what to do with it. Even if it was in any way appropriate. His younger brother, newly involved with one of their peers, had recently accused him of being dead from the neck down, and he hadn't exactly been wrong.

For the past year, he'd felt very little, aside from bouts of irritation and maybe a little paranoia, both of which served his purposes. Kept him sharp. He got irritated with people because stupidity and incompetence were pet peeves, and he paid close enough attention to his surroundings and everyone around him to stay safe, so he saw all the stupidity that went on. None of that inspired his libido.

Even before the shooting, he'd suspected violence and darkness lay at the heart of every person on the planet. That event had just driven the point home. Even the wide-eyed nurse practitioner changing in the other room had something wrong with her, deep down. Never mind her timid manner. Innocent masks were *still* masks.

He had darkness, he knew. Wolfe had it. Most people tried to fight that darkness, most of the time, or used coping mechanisms to cover it. Wolfe's jokes and sarcasm. His minute-by-minute reminder of the need for restraint and vigilance.

He checked his watch just as the second hand rounded twelve again. Three minutes past his two-minute limit.

No one took that long to change into scrubs. It was two simple pieces of clothing and a change of shoes.

He knocked on the door, as if it weren't a large public employee space, and before the sound had stopped resonating in the wood, his comm buzzed, a broadcast message immediately following. Four words.

All hands on deck.

His gut tightened.
All hands.
Departmental code for large-scale emergencies, when they expected to receive more patients than they were equipped to deal with. The kind of numbers that could only constitute a large group tragedy.

Right. Time for civility was past.

Decision made, he pushed into the locker room.

"Sabetta, what the devil is taking you so long?" He rounded the corner and found her wearing the scrub bottoms and shoes, but nothing above that save for a lacy pink bra that momentarily wiped his brain of any other thought besides the desire to stare, and absorb how delightful the pale pink lace looked against her tanned skin.

She had one foot braced against the locker beside hers, her blouse clamped between her elbow and her ribs, and both hands on the locker's latch, trying to wrench the thing open.

"It's stuck." She sounded breathless, as if she'd been fighting it for a while.

Slower than he'd like, his brain started to work again. He could either ask for details, spend time opening it himself or deal with it later.

All hands.

Deal with it later. That would get her clothed the fastest and time mattered.

"Put your top on," he bit out, dragging his gaze away, and opened his own locker instead of even attempting to wrestle hers into submission. As soon as he had it open, he began shoveling her things inside.

"If there's anything in here you need, speak now. We've got a large emergency to deal with. They've called all hands, which means even other departments send down whoever is free to assist. We need to go."

She stopped everything, maybe even breathing, for long enough that he had to look at her and found her eyes too wide again. And focused on him.

This was a mistake. She wasn't up for this.

Her eyes were rich chocolate, and the innocence he saw sucked him in. He protected others from danger, should he be protecting patients from her? Or her from rushing into the deep end before he knew she could swim?

Whatever she was thinking passed, and it really had only

been a couple of seconds before she started moving again, tugging her shirt in place and thrusting her hand into his locker to grab her stethoscope, a pen and her phone from her bag.

"I'm ready."

Another lie. But then again, it was the same lie he told himself every morning at the start of shift, when the double doors that cordoned off Emergency from the rest of the hospital felt like gates to a bloody battlefield where he was going to drag off bodies.

No. She wasn't ready. But he didn't have time to coddle her.

As soon as they hit the hallway, he sped up to run down the three turns it took to reach Emergency, with her following close behind.

Another thing he had no time for: dropping her off with Backeljauw to find a new sitter. That would have to come later.

No sooner had he reached the monitoring station than he had to step aside for a stretcher and team to roll past. The man on the stretcher had dark red compresses and bandages held to his abdomen. Conley headed the team, but, seeing him, nodded, which he took as a request to follow.

"Sabetta." He said her name, leaving her to figure out what she was supposed to do, and hurried off with the team.

Abdominal bleeding. A mass event. His mind could supply only one cause. Was this it, what his gut had been warning him about?

"Was it a shooting?" he asked Conley when he caught up, prompting her to begin her report there, since she was obviously wanting to hand the patient off. Pediatric emergencies were a little different from this kind of trauma.

A look flashed across her bonnie freckled face, confusion and then sympathy, but she shook her head. "Subway derailed. Yours is in triage."

She knew. His brother had obviously been sharing, and

Lyons didn't have the mental currency left to be angry about it.

Derailment. That could still be a man-made incident, but it wasn't a gun. It couldn't follow into the department and begin attacking personnel, unless it had been orchestrated and was the first step in a larger plan.

He turned, nearly trampling his unfortunate shadow, and had to grab her shoulders to stop them both making more of a mess of this. She grabbed his forearms in return, back to the wild-eyed stare as he took a breath and put her to the side to step around.

He pushed the tingle spreading from the center of his palms and hot on his arms from his head and jogged to meet the next stretcher coming out of triage.

Tingles didn't matter. The delicate, fragile-feeling slender shoulders on his new colleague didn't matter either. His too-young new colleague.

She kept up this time.

"What have we got?" he asked the nurses and paramedics rolling with his new patient.

"He was standing, and when it jumped track, he flew. Person from behind him hit him right after."

Crushing damage.

"Name?" Sabetta asked, reaching for the chart as they ran alongside the stretcher.

"Samuel Riggs."

"Mr. Riggs?" she called in his ear but got no response. "How long has he been unconscious?"

"Since it happened, probably. Uneven pupils, he's breathing too fast. Tachycardic," one of the paramedics filled in as they wheeled into the treatment bay.

"Get his shirt off." Lyons gloved and reached for his stethoscope.

She beat him to it, listening to the patient's heart while the others in the team fell in, taking the steps he didn't even need to order at this point. Get an IV started. Hook up the telemetry to monitor vitals.

A good sign, not freezing up as he'd half expected.

"Get a blood workup," he ordered, joining her in listening to the man's heart and lungs.

She'd grown a bit paler than she'd been, but that wasn't unusual for first-timers.

"Thoughts?" That would tell him more than blanching.

"His pulse is far too rapid," she answered, backing up the paramedic's report. "And he's heavily bruised. There's also a substantial lump on his head that I can see. If his pupils are unreactive, he needs a CT."

This was easier, working with a critical patient to take his focus.

Lyons listened again. Everyone breathed faster when tachycardic. The heart didn't pump blood and circulate oxygen efficiently, which caused the body's natural remedies to kick in, even if they couldn't help. He breathed faster naturally because his heart beat faster, it just didn't help.

"What's his pressure?"

One of his nurses took it manually while another worked on the telemetry and read off numbers far too low for his liking. She'd gotten the obvious things, and this wasn't a teaching hospital, but it was *his* hospital, and he needed to know his peers could handle themselves.

"What do you want to check?" He knew what he wanted to check, but he'd give her one shot since all the techs should be descending on the room any minute.

"Rapid heart and low blood pressure, along with all this bruising from the impact. I'd want to check for internal bleeding." She shook her head as she said it, as if she knew the answer was wrong, but stuck with it. "The head trauma is separate."

Right about the head trauma, wrong about the internal bleeding—which, while probably present, wasn't the most immediate danger to life.

"Look at his oxygen levels." He indicated with a nod.

A number in the high eighties; he could tell by her expression that she recognized it wasn't good.

"What tests?" he asked, giving her another shot.

"Typing for possible transfusion, a CBC, maybe troponin levels?"

Sticking with bleeding, but with a twist?

"Testing for heart attack?"

Wrong.

"All heart damage causes the same enzymes to release."

He waited for her to listen to the patient's chest one more time, still not leading.

She placed the bell to the man's chest and listened, but not to his lungs. Just his heart. It was the obvious symptom, the flashy thing demanding attention. When she commented again, it was on the speed, and shouldn't they slow it down? She'd somehow managed to miss that distinctive crackling sound his lungs made upon inspiration.

She'd said she normally worked Urgent Care facilities, not places that saw much active emergency. She wasn't ready for this, so out of her depth it was almost laughable. When he spoke to Backeljauw, he'd suggest she be shifted to the non-emergency cases.

"I want a CT, head and chest. Image and circulation." He directed his team. "And a blood panel. At least one lung has been damaged. I want a D-dimer."

"For clotting?" she asked.

"Go back to the station and wait." He grabbed his comm to suggest to Imaging that they hurry the hell up, but as she stood, looking confused, added for her benefit, "I don't have time to hold your hand through this. Neither does he."

CHAPTER THREE

STICKING AROUND TO defend herself or make excuses would've taken valuable time away from the patient, so Belle did as McKeag growled at her, slipped quietly out of the room and found her way back to the nurses' station.

Her central nervous system couldn't decide how to react to that whole humiliating set-down. Her face alternated between burning at a temperature best measured in Kelvin and the stormfront of an approaching Ice Age any time she relived the joy of the actual rebuke, and the number of eyes on her, the team working as she failed her first patient.

Still, with the hospital in the throes of a large-scale emergency, standing there, observing the bustle and scurrying about without helping somehow could be nothing short of dereliction of duty.

She wasn't a doctor. She wasn't trained for this type of medicine or level of emergency straight out of the gate and had truly only offered her best educated guess when prompted, but it still felt the same when an expert—a peer—immediately found her lacking. Even one she knew to be unpleasant in other circumstances already.

Something about it had felt like a *teaching* moment, but, in retrospect, she could see it had been a test. An unfair test, the kind of test only a real jerk would lob at a new colleague in the first five minutes on the floor, but still a test she'd failed.

It wasn't just pride that never wanted to fail a patient. Not everyone went into medicine for the right reasons, but Belle had. Her main role models had been Dad and Nanna, a city cop and a former Army nurse. Belle wanted to *help* people, it was a core tenet of her personality. Seeing the nurses who'd taken care of not only her dad as he'd lingered in the days between when the bullets had wrecked his insides and when he'd actually died, but also the fourteen-year-old girls who couldn't leave his side, had solidified that need to help into a calling.

And she was just standing around, while other people helped eased suffering.

If this was just how things went in a large, metropolitan emergency department, she had to either get out now and make this a one-day affair or find that steel Sabetta core and a way to help.

Like a gift from a higher power, the woman they'd initially followed passed by the nurses' station, a light at the end of the tunnel. Belle stood and gave chase. She'd directed McKeag earlier; she'd have ideas on where Belle could be of use.

"Doctor?" Belle called.

The woman spun to face her as if she'd been expecting her call.

"Ysabelle?" Her smile and the soft southern cadence of her speech seemed to project sunshine from her pretty, freckled face and blazingly blue eyes.

For a moment, Belle even stopped mentally cursing McKeag to a lifetime of stubbing his right pinky toe any time he tried to go shoeless and enjoy the simple pleasure of the earth beneath his feet. This doctor was the exact opposite to McKeag's surly presence—someone Belle could identify with.

"I'm Dr. Angel Conley, and we're going to be working together today." She offered a hand. "Do you prefer to be called Ysabelle or Sabetta? You can call me Angel."

"Belle," she managed to get out, then shook the offered hand. "Dr. McKeag wanted me to wait, but—"

"Yeah, Lyons is— Well, he doesn't work and play well with others." Angel added, "But I'm sure we can make the request for you to stay with him if you want. Between you and me? I'd rather shadow an angry mule than Lyons when he's on a tear. Which is nearly always."

The gentle teasing confidence gave a little shot of hope to counter the increasingly awful rot in her chest.

Belle squeezed Angel's hand, needing exactly that connection in that moment—she'd have hugged this stranger if she could've—it seemed the only thing to go in her favor since she'd arrived in New York. But still. "I'm not sure he should receive all the blame here. I apparently went the entirely wrong direction with the patient."

"We all have our specialties, and I'm sure we'll find yours," Angel said, gesturing for her to follow. "I'm a pediatric emergency specialist. Kids are my specialty, but I still need the help of trauma surgeons in unfortunate instances. Or cardiac specialists. We have a network. But we'll talk more about this later. How are you with stitching?"

"I'm good at stitching," Belle said and, with just the simple act of reminding herself that she did have strengths, amended, "I'm actually very good at stitching. If I had my education to do over again, I'd probably become a surgeon. I'm good with my hands."

And with patients, she reminded herself. She'd become a nurse because she needed to take care of people, and she was good at connecting. She made mistakes, and she didn't know everything, but she cared and connected, she *tried*. And would *keep* trying.

"Perfect. We have a heavy load today because of a subway derailment, which you probably heard, but not all the injuries are critical. Most of them are much more minor. Cuts. Sprains. Broken bones."

Even with the little mental pep talk, she must've looked

off still because Angel stepped closer, her voice lowering. "I know what it's like to be new and feel disconnected from everyone. Don't let Lyons scare you off. He's—" She paused, obviously searching for some polite way to describe the arrogant doctor. "Christmas is hard for him. There are extenuating circumstances. Just take whatever he says with a grain of salt, and if you have trouble with anything, come see me. Do you have your comm yet?"

Christmas was *hard* for him. Even among the other things Angel said, that was what stood out.

The words resonated in Belle's head, bouncing off her guilt centers and disrupting her presently cursing him to a month of upper lip and tongue burns from the morning's first over-eager sip of too-hot coffee. It took effort to focus on the other important things Angel had said.

"I'm supposed to get it this afternoon. They said I wouldn't need it since I'd be shadowing today," Belle said, ceasing her ever ineffective but frequently cathartic cursing because it'd been useless at soothing her ruffled feathers.

Christmas was *hard* for him. Hard enough to affect his behavior. It hurt him.

He lashed out because he was suffering.

"Right. Well, you're shadowing me. I'm just going to be in and out with a couple other patients while you stitch. But if you need anything, come to me. Really. I've almost been here a year, but I've pretty much sorted out the people to see to get things done. I also know all the best places to hide if you need a minute to practice a completely silent, faux primal scream because they might sedate you if you actually let your feelings out."

"My locker." Belle wanted to laugh at the image of her screaming soundlessly into some cabinet because she was stressing out, but facing Lyons again was right there in the front of her mind, taking the humor out of living. "My locker is stuck. The emergency call came, and McKeag tossed my things into his locker so we could get down here. It'd be really nice to have it working for tomorrow."

It wouldn't save her facing him this evening to get her stuff back, but it would allow her to start tomorrow with some distance.

"I can do that. What's the number?"

A moment later, Angel was on her comm, walking off in the other direction, and Belle had a folder in hand, and slipped into the room of a man with a large leg gash to stitch.

"Hi, my name is Ysabelle Sabetta and I'm a nurse practitioner. I'm going to help you get that gash sorted out," she said to the man sitting with his trouser leg ripped open and a bloody wad of gauze keeping it from bleeding too much. After confirming his identity, she got started.

"Please numb it." Mr. Axler said three words to her, and then laid back on the table. No comments on her qualifications or ability to do the job, no doubts.

In that way, outside the jerky way he'd gone about it, McKeag had a point. People accepted you'd be able to help them when you came in wearing scrubs. They deserved that confidence.

Washing up, she gloved, got supplies—some of which had been laid out for her by nursing staff—and moved over to get a look at what was going on with the patient's leg.

Christmas was *hard* for McKeag. It was still there in her head, behind her duties to her patient, but still there.

She didn't want it.

She gingerly lifted the bloody gauze to see beneath, causing her patient to draw a sharp, pained breath. It hurt; she knew it hurt.

"I'm sorry. I know it's hard, but I need you to be still for this. I'll be as gentle as I can to make it as easy as possible, but it'll go quicker and cleaner if you lock that leg in place as best you can."

That was part of her job, even if it wasn't technically

codified in rules of conduct—to make the painful things easier for those who were suffering.

Christmas was hard for McKeag. She'd seen that. Anyone could see that. But hearing Angel put it into words—now she couldn't hold his behavior against him. Couldn't curse him to a lifetime of mushy pasta or underwear that snuck into uncomfortable arrangements at inopportune moments.

Before Angel, he'd just been someone who hated the holiday, now he was someone *struggling* with it.

An important difference. If she'd had any distance, she should've seen that on her own. Nanna had said it to her and Noelle so many times, it was practically a family mantra, even if it'd started out as a way to explain to two hurt little girls why their mother had left them.

Words said to make them understand it wasn't their fault, because they didn't remember her.

People who hurt others needed extra kindness to get better.

Their mother's life had been too hard and her family too bad for her to know how to be a mother. Nanna made sure they understood Mama had become someone who didn't really know how to love. That it was a tragedy she'd given up before all the love they and Dad had to give could transform her into the person she was always meant to be.

People who hurt others needed extra kindness.

Mama had been too far gone for quick fixes, and even now Belle couldn't bring herself to consider looking for her. She wasn't steady enough on her feet to take on that kind of damage. Besides, it felt like a betrayal to Noelle, who couldn't make that choice anymore.

Was McKeag too far gone too?

The gash on her patient's leg was deep but flayed open with remarkable precision. It barely grazed the muscle beneath; the only part that needed stitching was the cleanly sliced skin that now stood open.

She *had* a patient. *This* patient. The one with a wound she knew she could stitch.

She pulled a light down to see into the wound better, selecting one with a magnifying window so she could be certain the wound was cleaned out before she began stitching it.

Maybe the person who had included McKeag in that gift thing had been trying to be kind to him. Not a bad idea, but the execution was problematic. A gift exchange forced him to do something in exchange for his gift, which wasn't what someone reticent to participate in the season needed.

She picked out a couple of little pieces of glass with tweezers. "I want to flush this with saline, Mr. Axler, to make sure it's clean before I stitch it. I'm going to go ahead and numb it, so it's easier on you when I work a towel underneath your leg."

"Whatever you think. Just want to go through this once."

"The shot will be the most painful part. A few quick sticks, and I apologize. I'll make them as quickly as I can," she said, prepping the needle and scoping out locations to numb.

"Were you by yourself on the subway this morning?" Distraction was a useful technique for dealing with pain, and she'd use anything to save patients from pain.

"I was on my way to work."

She injected twice during his answer, his words only pausing or faltering a second for each injection.

"Are you married?"

"Yes."

"Have kids?"

"Two."

She finished the last injection and stood up to look down at him. "Injections over, should be feeling better any second. Boys? Girls?"

"One of each," he said a little more easily, his voice letting her know it was working. Not only did talking help by distracting, but it provided a connection that soothed fear.

She found a couple of towels in a cabinet, got them under his leg and had flushed the wound to her satisfaction by the time Angel came in.

"How's it going?"

"There was a little glass in the wound, but it's clean now. I'm about to stitch it up."

"Great. I'll go to my next patient and pop back over when I'm done."

"Is this your first day?" Mr. Axler asked.

"It's my first day at this facility, but I've been doing this for several years now," Belle answered, smiling at him. "I was an RN before I went back to school. Even if I look like a kid."

"You do look young." He chuckled but relaxed back.

She kept him talking as she worked. How did he meet his wife? How old were their children? Was she coming to pick him up at the hospital after this?

It worked. It usually did, and by the time she had him stitched and bandaged, that horrible anxiety from earlier had stopped chewing up her insides.

She met Angel back at the monitoring station, where another nurse walked her through the hospital's patient system, so the file could be updated. Then they were off to another patient.

The morning continued this way, interspersed with patients and thoughts of McKeag. What had happened to him? Was he grieving too? Or trying not to grieve, like her?

By the time lunch rolled around, the worst of the influx had been handled and Angel returned to seeing strictly children with Belle shadowing.

Being busy always kept her from dwelling too much on the stuff she didn't need to dwell on. This morning's failure. Her reasons for coming to New York. The way Christmas now had a mood more suited to Halloween, but instead of ghosts and goblins, it was Christmas trees with teeth and murderous tinsel.

Getting around the department meant she also saw Mc-Keag growling at three other people before the day was up. Which helped shore up her resolve. It also helped negate her earlier estimation of his attractiveness. She might see and understand that he was wounded, and she might want to help him, but it did take the shine off his good looks and make his jaw seem less chiseled, more brutish.

He needed someone to be kind to him, maybe even more than she needed someone to be kind to, to give gifts to this Christmas in New York when she should've been buying for her twin.

Because she did need it and wanted to give to someone who might be a colleague for years to come. Someone she might be able to see change.

Whatever the true definition of the twelve days of Christmas, she'd learned last year that the lead-up to the holiday was the hardest to get through.

There were twelve more days left before Christmas Day. He might not be working that whole time, and she certainly wouldn't be, but it had a kind of symmetry to it that appealed to her, even if she only managed to get him a few secret gifts before he took holiday.

She'd give to him, her stand-in Noelle, an act her family would've been proud of. After work and on weekends, she'd visit the quintessential New York Christmas sites to get the pictures she'd need to write to Noelle about, another unnecessary, yet wholly necessary, act.

That was how she'd survive Christmas this year. This second year alone had to be better than the first had been; she couldn't do that again.

At the end of her shift, as soon as she could safely see to the handling of her last patient, Belle made her way back to the locker room.

Lyons, which she'd decided to think of him now in an

effort to separate him from the feelings she had about Mc-Keag, would be irritated if she made him wait for her.

Even with her new plan of action, the idea of facing him made her nerves tangle.

He'd still been with a patient when she'd exited Emergency so she could have time to test her locker door to be sure it had been fixed before he arrived.

Now all she had to do was get her things from Lyons and try to establish a new tone for their conversation, because his reformation couldn't hinge entirely on gifts—he needed kind human interaction too. A friend. Or at least someone he had a less contentious relationship with than he seemed to have with all their colleagues. Earlier, she'd been nervous, which could've only come across as weakness. He was not a man who appreciated weakness, no question. She hoped that meant he'd be the kind of man who appreciated people trying to better themselves.

She didn't have to go to medical school to learn more of what she might expect in a busy, big city emergency department and be better prepared. This wasn't the same as an Urgent Care, and *maybe* her skills had gotten rusty in those gentle positions.

If she could inspire that in him, maybe it would trickle out to his interactions with everyone else and he'd stop yelling so much and make the department easier for everyone. Even if he wasn't in charge, he still seemed to see everyone as an underling who continuously disappointed him.

Noelle would've told her to be bold, to confront him and tell him that she wouldn't be pushed around. Noelle had always been the brave one, never afraid of confrontation. The first year she'd been a pilot, she'd had to suffer fools daily who hadn't thought a woman could safely handle an airplane.

Belle was the introverted twin—which confused her really. The whole nature-or-nurture debate went nuclear when it came to the two of them, people who shared the same

DNA and were raised in exactly the same way, but who were closer to two opposite halves of one complete person than identical twins.

Had been.

She was doing it again, dwelling on a subject that always stripped away shreds of her composure until she was a raw mass of emotional hamburger.

The door to the locker room squeaked, and she cleared her throat and swallowed down the unwelcome surge of grief, turning in time to see Lyons rounding the bank of lockers in the middle—in much the same fashion as he'd done this morning in HR: as if it never occurred to him that someone could be in his way. Or wouldn't move once they saw him.

"Here you are." His accent was a little more present, she noticed immediately. His words less clipped. Perhaps he'd shouted himself out? Or perhaps it was just her impression of him, and how she was trying to change it.

"You were still with a patient, and I wanted to come up and make certain Maintenance had unstuck my locker." She crooked a thumb toward the now repaired thing. "So, you won't have to deal with the clutter of extra clothing tomorrow. Thank you for the loan of your space today."

He stopped and stared as soon as he saw her face, his brows slamming down above those icy eyes. No words came, he just scowled while searching her face.

Her lashes were damp, she realized. Must've not stopped the tears in time to keep him from seeing the piece her memories had freshly ripped out. She'd thought she'd gotten control of herself in time, but even with her tanned skin, her eyebrows and nose had a tendency to go red, even before the actual tears gathered. That was probably the tell.

What surprised her was how long he took deciding what to do, or maybe think, about it.

She willed him not to ask, and, although she had to draw

the last ounce of today's strength reserves, lifted her chin and held his gaze, daring him to bring it up.

It was only a second, and he didn't so much back down as decide to move on. He opened his locker and began fishing out her belongings. "It was no trouble."

She didn't actually snort. At least on the outside.

"I suppose it was less trouble than I was otherwise." She took the still-packaged scrubs and the tote bag her clothing had been stashed in and began sorting it out for her ride home. Before he answered, she added, "About that, I don't know if I'll see that exact situation again, but I'd like to prepare myself better for it. For all this. I was wondering if you had suggestions on texts to read."

He pulled his top off, leaving the white tee shirt beneath it, and dropped the worn shirt onto the bench in front of his locker. Unfortunately, a snug cotton shirt only made his impressive torso more impressive. The material clung; she could mark the shape of each muscle across the top of his back and shoulders. "Any texts on emergency treatment. Field treatment texts are actually a good start. The Army has a good one available."

He shook out a nice dress shirt, pulled it on and began buttoning it up.

It was weird to stand there talking while he changed, and she refused to—unlike he-of-the-impressive-shoulders, she didn't have a tee shirt beneath her scrub top and having him see her in her bra once was plenty.

Without the scrubs, it was easier to see him as Lyons, not Dr. McKeag. It also made her earlier attempts to convince herself he wasn't really attractive completely ridiculous. He was handsome, but his face was also interesting. A study in angles, juxtaposed with a generous, soft mouth. Noelle could've had a field day drawing him—because being a brave warrior for women's rights hadn't been enough, her sister had also been able to work magic with a pencil.

The burning returned.

She had to get out of there. Stay on task. This was supposed to be about improving his impression of her and doing whatever she needed to become better equipped at dealing with her new duties, not having an emotional breakdown. She dug her fingers into the side of her thigh to give focus, and asked, "Earlier, what did I miss?"

"His lungs, the crackling in his breath sounds. You were dazzled by the heart," he answered immediately, finished buttoning his shirt, then turned more fully toward her. "The heart rate was a symptom of pulmonary contusion. They found an embolism that formed where the bruise had nearly collapsed it. So, he had both."

Yeah, pulmonary contusion, she hadn't ever seen that, but she couldn't find fault with his critique. She *had* been dazzled by the excessively fast heart rate and blinded by her own idea of what internal bleeding would look like.

"Do you know how he's doing?"

"He is in ICU, still unconscious."

He'd kept up with the status of a patient who was no longer under his care. That was the sign she'd been hoping for—he was in the profession to help people. Whatever his unpleasant exterior—his demeanor and words—there was goodness there somewhere. Maybe it wasn't too late.

"His head trauma?"

"That's the reason he's still unconscious." He looked in his locker for a moment, took out a pair of trousers, then hung them on the corner of the locker door, apparently waiting until their conversation was over to finish changing. Bless him. She didn't need to see more of his impressive parts.

"Diagnosis?"

"Diffuse brain injury," Lyons answered, and still his voice remained even, almost gentle. This wasn't just her reframing their interaction; he was more at ease now. "I don't expect him to wake. He's on steroids in the hopes of shrinking the swelling, but he's also vented. We'll know more in the next couple of days."

She seemed to have done what she'd planned, now she should get out. The sooner she left, the sooner he could dress and leave, and the sooner she could return and commence Operation: Secret Santa.

"I'm glad he had you," she said finally, swinging her coat on and hoisting the tote bag to her shoulder to go.

"Sabetta?"

She'd reached the bank of lockers when she heard her name and turned to look back at him. He still had that stoic, measuring manner, but with his arms uncrossed he didn't look as forbidding. He looked almost open. And even with the strange scrubs-and-button-down-shirt combination, she could tell he could devastate half the female population by putting on a suit.

"If you have questions about diagnoses, you may ask them of me. Use the comm."

She felt herself smile before she knew it was coming. "Thank you. I will. And I'll go home and start reading. I don't have anything on the schedule tonight in terms of sightseeing."

"Sightseeing?"

Was he actually being polite? Even if the subject was hard, a glimpse of civility gave her hope.

"I'm taking pictures of Christmas in New York to send to my sister."

"Not going home for the holidays?"

"No." She shook her head, falling back into the usual way she spoke of Noelle—the only way that let her keep any control over her emotions: by using the present tense. "We usually go somewhere for Christmas, no other family. But not this year."

"Perhaps next year." Polite, but the words he'd said in kindness stuck in her chest. There would be no next year.

No looking forward to things Noelle would never do. The trips they'd never take. The children she'd never have.

The polite thing for her to do would be to ask if he was going home for the holidays, but her throat had clogged with the boulders of everything that could never be and filled with the sands of regret and grief, feelings she always tried to keep shoved down. It would've also been polite to say goodnight now, but no sound could pass through the whole world blocking her dry throat.

All she could do, all she had been doing for more than a year, was try and put it out of her mind until later.

Besides, she had tasks to accomplish. Tonight, she'd start simple, visit the boutique coffee shop near the hospital's gift shop for a gift card, and pray it fit through the vents on the front of his locker.

Then she'd have the weekend to come up with other gifts she could shove through the narrow openings.

CHAPTER FOUR

Friday morning arrived with a winter storm, and Lyons credited the accumulating snowfall with the lightening of his mood, even if it also just made his drive to the hospital perilous.

Most people reacted negatively when heavy snow started to fall, but in Lyons's experience, weather affected the variety of patients they saw for the *better*. Shifted the balance from man-made to bad Fate: natural causes or accidents.

Injuries were injuries, logically he knew that, but he'd rather blame the whims of Fate for tragedies to befall a person or family than another situation where he was forced to question humanity. Cold enough weather even encouraged psychopaths to stay in and commit their atrocities on a warmer day.

He stomped his boots on the rug inside the rear entrance of the hospital, knocking off as much fresh powder as he could before heading to the locker room.

Yesterday had been a bad Fate day, a terrible accident by all accounts, but the whole day, he'd been unable to shake the suspicion that someone had caused it. Done something to the train. Messed with the track or the electronics that ran the system. Something.

No one had even hinted at such a situation, but it had still taken him until late in the evening, long after he'd left Sutcliffe, to convince himself he was being paranoid, that no reasonable person would jump to that conclusion with no basis or evidence. That kind of reaction was the stuff of conspiracy theories and unstable minds. Lizard-people-controlling-the-government-videos-online-level paranoia.

But knowing he was *probably* being paranoid didn't make the idea he was being foolish comforting, or certain. Ten percent of *What if?* was stronger than ninety percent of *No way* in the moment, when even that measly ten percent could result in loss of life.

Before the shooting, he'd never thought that way. Not without cause. Certainly, his wretched, emotionally abusive and manipulative parents had inadvertently taught him people were inherently selfish and would use anyone to get what they wanted, but the idea that someone he knew would take that to the point of murder? Couldn't happen. Not to him. Not to someone he knew and cared about.

It was stupid.

Every day he saw people who never thought it could happen to them dealing with terrible tragedies, but he still would've never believed Eleni's husband—a man he'd socialized with at hospital events—could turn *that* violent. Even after she'd confided in him about the abuse and had come to the hospital that day to finally take Lyons up on his offer of helping her get out, he hadn't thought something like that possible.

That kind of violence was cowardly, and something usually hidden from public view, not the kind that showed up with a gun in a busy ER on Christmas Eve.

He hadn't thought it could happen to anyone he knew. Not to her. And that was on him.

He jerked opened the door to the locker room, shedding his heavy coat en route to his locker. Early. He always came in early enough to overlap the previous shift by at least an hour, because he couldn't have another situation like that on him again. He went over the roster of patients, peeked into rooms to see who might set off his internal alarms and kept a sharp eye.

He had to pay better attention than he'd paid at Ramapo Memorial.

If he'd understood the likelihood of an escalation of the violence, he'd have taken precautions. It would've never gotten to the point of a madman loose in his ER with a gun. He'd have sent her to his home instead, which was well guarded and safer. He'd have directed hospital security to keep out anyone not authorized to be back there, even spouses and known family. If he'd understood how those kinds of situations could leapfrog over occasional hitting and frequent emotional abuse to murder, he'd have gone about it differently, he wouldn't have had to step in front of a bullet only to have his friend die anyway, and he would've gotten the police involved early, no matter how fervently she'd pleaded with him not to.

All good reasons to pay attention now and keep in the front of his mind what happened when he let his guard down.

He rounded the bank of lockers and stumbled, blind luck allowing him to catch himself before he went down.

Sabetta had come in early—earlier than him—and now sat on the bench in front of her locker, attention buried in her phone.

Unlike yesterday, today she seemed fully ready to begin her shift. Thank God. Not half dressed. Less of a strange, unexpected temptation. Theoretically. But that lock of hair still hung free in the front, begging to be tucked back, looking unreasonably silky…

He had to figure out how to handle her. Whether to say something about the day before. He probably should. He came to Sutcliffe to work, not to make friends or win some kind of popularity contest, but he also didn't like knowing he was entirely in the wrong in a situation. He'd also realized last night how big an ass he'd been to her.

"You're early," he said, jerking her attention from her phone, her expression making clear she hadn't even been aware that he'd entered when he was standing not five feet away from her. The urge to apologize started to fade, replaced by a desire to lecture her about the importance of being aware of her surroundings. Situational awareness was something every New Yorker should learn, but especially those who worked or lived in areas where violence could break out unexpectedly. Like a hospital.

"Morning." She turned her phone off and sat up straighter, brows pinching as she clearly took a minute to mentally right herself. "I thought the commute would take longer. I also thought my locker door might be sticking again and I'd need to get Maintenance."

"So, you weren't hanging out here to see me." He tried to joke, but the rapid shake of her head said she didn't hear it as a joke.

"It was just quiet in here, and out of the way," she said, already moving, already running away. Not the time to apologize for unfairly treating her, clearly. "The cafeteria will be open, and my body wants caffeine."

He unlocked the locker, then turned to reiterate that she could ask him questions if she needed to, but she was already gone.

He jerked the door of his locker open and something fell out, then slid under the bench behind him.

His heart fell, the déjà vu instantly turning his mood around. Snow might keep psychopaths indoors, but not people from shoving junk into his locker. He should tape the damned vents.

He slammed his bag into the locker, finishing what he was doing before he dealt with yet another Christmas irritation. It had to be related; it fell like a card. Yesterday's paper had fluttered, this had flopped and slid, weightier and smaller, more compact.

Once he'd collected the various paraphernalia he carried

on his shift and sorted them into the appropriate pockets, he bent over to retrieve what had fallen.

Small white envelope. Thick. Heavy. Like the boulder in his gut.

He swore under his breath, immediately glad Sabetta had slipped out. She'd already seen him lose his cool once over this holiday nonsense, although it might make it easier to keep his hands to himself—something that seemed strangely difficult—if she thought him off enough to avoid.

An idea that disgruntled almost as much as another damned Christmas reminder.

He flipped the envelope over, but found no writing, just thick folded paper.

It was small, but heavier than a greeting card. Invitation maybe?

He could throw it out, throw it back or look inside.

Probably a flipping wedding invitation. He'd been trying to dissuade his little brother from rushing in, even gone so far as to remind him about the carnage caused by their parents' marriage, but Wolfe either had chosen to forget, or didn't care. A diamond ring had gotten involved no matter Lyons's helpful advice.

Or another dinner invitation from either of them, in more formal means. Since they'd decided they were blissfully in love with each other and the season, they'd each invited him over for dinner at least once each. Wolfe had done it twice, on the phone and in person. A Christmas card would almost be more welcome at this point.

Get on with it.

Decision made, he flicked the seal open and drew out a generic "Season's Greetings" card and found a holiday gift card inserted into little slits inside, the name of the little coffee shop downstairs on the front.

He could feel his blood pressure rising.

There were lines intended to be filled out with gifting information, and they were empty. Nothing personal to identify the gift-giver. No one to shout at.

And not a threat, just a reminder of the worst day of his life, which always managed to feel like a threat. Not a threat. Nothing dangerous about it. No matter what the adrenalin spike jittering through his system said.

He repeated the sentiment to himself twice, a habit he'd had to increase since the month rolled to December.

It was just a gift card. A thin slice of plastic with cheerful gold letters and holly leaves. He carefully breathed out and laid the card on the shelf in his locker while regrouping.

Could be Wolfe, but his brother would sign his name.

Could be Conley. She might not sign her name because their relationship, whatever it might be, was more tenuous.

Sabetta?

He glanced down the bench to where she'd been sitting.

An apology, perhaps? Ineffective without a name attached. No, Conley was the most likely suspect. Conley, whom Wolfe had told about last Christmas.

The tension in his head spread over his whole scalp.

But he should still react more civilized than he felt like acting, because that reaction was never going to be socially appropriate. Especially not work appropriate.

Civilized. Take the card. Use it to buy himself and Conley a coffee later. Thank her. Let that be the end of it.

The deck was already stacked against Wolfe's relationship, and he wouldn't add to it. Plus, he was a little relieved Wolfe wasn't rushing into the wedding, regardless of what the ring said. He'd tried to talk some sense into Wolfe before it came to declarations and cohabitation decisions, and that hadn't worked. This was one thing he could not protect his little brother from, but he wouldn't do anything to speed it along.

One more deep breath and he stashed the card in his pocket, closed everything up and went to make a check of the department. Even with the weather as his ally this morning, he couldn't begin a shift without identifying all the possible threats.

Christmas messed things up, and somehow people were surprised when it happened. Not him. Not anymore.

Belle shuffled forward two paces in the lunch line at the cafeteria. It was longer today than yesterday—no one seemed to want to brave the driving snow to get something less institutional-tasting.

The increased number of people around her ramped up the already high stress levels clinging to her. And would've even if she weren't wary of consequences to her Secret Santa program.

She'd spent the entire morning looking over her shoulder, expecting Lyons to figure her out and then come murder her with a shiv he'd spent the morning fashioning out of the gift card.

Or just disdainfully stare her to death. If anyone could murder with a look, it would be that man and his ice-cold eyes.

She definitely shouldn't carry on with this gifting business on Monday. Last night, she'd spent the evening brainstorming flat, small, skinny gift ideas and mostly coming up with gift cards. Or tea bags she shoved through the vents one at a time—obviously a great idea. After a couple of hours, she gave up and admitted she'd have to rely on the Christmas spirit of her peers and leave the gifts outside his locker should she choose to continue. She just wasn't sure she should choose.

When she'd slipped the card into his locker, she hadn't left any indication of who'd bought it. No words. No promises of more days. No fingerprints. Because she watched true crime documentaries and had an overactive imagination that went wild considering the lengths Lyons would go to for retribution against the gift-giver.

She wanted to ask someone for advice.

She wanted to ask her sister.

Noelle would have an opinion. And her opinion would probably be to continue doing the brave thing, even if Belle seemed to have somehow missed the brave gene during gestation. It all went to Noelle, while Belle got the be quiet and say 'please' and 'thank you' gene. And Lyons had already decreed he'd gotten the oft misunderstood Scottish Sarcasm Gene. Which was kind of funny, in a dry sort of way. Probably the only joke he'd ever told.

Again, the line inched forward.

She could just leave this off, focus her time elsewhere for the holidays, because that part had not changed. She needed a Christmas-shaped distraction. She needed all the distractions, really. And having only been at Sutcliffe all of two days now, she knew two things very well: every single person in the department was nervous or standoffish of Lyons, and the hospital wasn't going to let her do overtime on the weekends until she'd established herself. So sometime after the holidays. When she'd have much less interest in an overtime distraction. The only other after-hours jobs she'd been able to think of were in retail, and after the days in a Manhattan ER, she wasn't sure she could handle Christmas shoppers.

Better she focus on the New York Christmas experience. Get pictures to send to Noelle rather than writing another hour-long diatribe about her day at work and the pathetic little picture of the gift card she'd taken before playing insane postman.

She turned her attention to her phone, and the maps of the public transportation system. Where could she go after work for a photo that wouldn't take too long to get to, and also wouldn't be risking life and limb in the snow?

"Sabetta."

The hair on the back of her neck stood up and Belle

looked over her shoulder to see the man in question, and all desire to eat her lunch dropped like some internal anvil, right through the organ previously demanding food. Loudly. At inconvenient moments. With patients.

This was it. He was here to skillfully carve her heart out with a sharpened spork.

"Dr. Lyons," she said, and then blinked and coughed. "I mean, Dr. McKeag. I'm... Forgive me. I learned your first name today, and it's also a last name, kind of got my wires crossed."

He looked at her a little strangely but shrugged it off. "I've been called worse."

Probably daily.

"Still." She gestured in front of her, offering the spot in line. That would both allow her to keep an eye on him and avoid wasting any of his time, which she already knew he disliked.

"No, that's fine. Ladies first." He looked far too relaxed, at least compared to yesterday, which was her only point of comparison. Work McKeag was a grenade with the key half-pulled, After Work Lyons could carry on this style of conversation with no yelling, no growling, no icy death-glares. He actually looked in a good mood still. Maybe yesterday had just been an off day?

Or maybe his day had been improved by the little gift left to greet him this morning.

The thought bloomed so deeply, she actually felt physically lighter, as if a breath of warm, tropical air filled her chest.

She stepped forward and he stepped up behind her—not difficult since she was at the very end of the line—letting her hide her goofy smile she felt but couldn't seem to banish. He'd liked the little gift. It had been a nothing gift, but the kindness of it. This was going to be okay, to be a good thing for him.

* * *

Lyons had considered, briefly, what to say when next he saw Sabetta.

I treated you unfairly...you can shadow me if you like.

Simple. To the point. Not infested with either emotion or too much welcome, so maybe she'd not take him up on it but the courtesy would salve somewhat.

He opened his mouth to say so, but something made him pause. Small talk was something Lyons hated on principle. Small talk meant nothing to him and didn't ever convey anything of substance. It was a waste of time and breath.

But...maybe he should say *something* to her before just blurting out the invitation. Ease the way. Although, that might encourage her to take it.

Would it be so bad to *encourage* her to take him up on it? Nothing too dangerous could happen if he kept his focus...

Before he worked out what he actually wanted to say, what result he wanted, she'd returned to ignoring him and the entire world around her in favor of staring at her phone. Again.

He tilted his head to see what she was doing. Not texting. Tracking a subway line along a map.

"Are you planning a shopping excursion?" he asked, breaking the silence again as they shuffled forward toward the actual food and not miles of trays and silverware.

"I'm looking for somewhere to go get a picture."

She didn't look at him, just kept scrolling around, flipping back and forth between screens in between telling the worker behind the counter what she wanted on her sandwich and what kind of soup to dish up.

And didn't explain what she meant at all.

"A picture of what?"

"A Christmas picture. For my sister. I already sent a Rockefeller Center tree picture to her the day before yesterday, but yesterday I didn't get out anywhere to get a good picture."

He gave his order quickly, then turned to look over his shoulder to the bank of windows separating the ground-floor cafeteria from the patio, where people could sit and eat when the temperatures weren't made of frosty death.

Presently, all he could see was the vague outline of furniture through the driving snow and the blue cast everything took from the wintry onslaught.

"Going anywhere to get pictures in this is ridiculous," he muttered. Helpfully. It was helpful to tell people they were being stupid if it was to their benefit to be told. Caring. Protective. "And obviously not something you're excited about—you're scowling into your phone."

"No, I'm not." Her voice had a sharpness he hadn't heard before, and which seemed out of proportion to his mild observation. Even when he'd snapped at her, her response had been even and measured...

She stashed her phone in her pocket, took the dishes handed to her over the protective glass casing, then moved closer to the cashier, saying nothing else. But if shoulders could have a tone, hers did. A sharp tone. She stood so stiffly he wanted to touch her, jostle her, put her back to rights.

But he also wanted to make her see sense. "Tell your sister to come visit you if she's so demanding of the New York Christmas experience."

The words were barely out, and she turned to glare at him. Her dark eyes, which seemed vulnerable and far too young every other time he'd looked at her, now drilled into him. He'd been an ass to her and she hadn't looked like that. So baleful.

Damn. This was not how this was supposed to go.

And he cared, for some reason. Maybe because she hadn't written him off even after he'd been a jerk. Maybe it was a protective instinct. He had no idea. But it had been a long time since he'd thought of anyone in a positive light.

A long time since he'd even been tempted to believe the best in anyone. Or wanted anyone to believe the best in him.

"I've got that," he said over her shoulder to the cashier. "This is together."

"No, it's not." She waved a hand at the woman ringing up their lunch. "We're not together."

"We're not together," he echoed, but added, "but I am paying for both lunches. It's… It's a… Christmas…thing. Merry Christmas."

He didn't know where the words came from, and clearly neither did Sabetta, who appeared so thrown by his statement that she stopped arguing. Her eyes rounded and stopped the neon *Go to hell* sign he'd seen there. For a second, she almost looked *happy*, of all things.

It took her almost as long to answer as it had taken him to sputter the words out. "Thank you. Merry Christmas to you too."

She grabbed her tray and fled, weaving through the tables at lightning speed in an obvious attempt to get away from him.

Buying lunch wasn't going to make up any ground, even as much as his *Merry Christmas* had. And he wasn't finished. He had a half-formed plan to complete.

He paid quickly, keeping an eye on the tables to see which way she headed, and set out after her as soon as the money left his hand.

It only took a moment to find her in the thickly packed tables. She'd chosen a small table, out of the way, and sat with her back to the room. A terrible habit. A dangerous habit. And it was his moral responsibility to say something, even if it made her angrier.

"If you're trying to run away from me, you shouldn't sit in such a manner that it's easy for me to sneak up on you," he said as he put his tray on the table beside hers and sat. "I'm trying to be friendly."

She grabbed the edges of her seat and gave a little hop,

and then another, opening up a little distance between them at the small table. "You just called me stupid for trying to make my Christmas away from my sister more bearable."

Her words took a bite out of his righteous indignation and the distancing technique shamed him. If the cafeteria weren't packed, he had no doubt she'd move to a different table. Still might, by the look of her, if he didn't fix this.

"You're right. I'm out of practice making conversation, and I hate talking small." He took a moment to consider how to continue and took it as a good sign that she didn't flee. "I didn't mean to belittle your difficulties, but everyone is their own kind of miserable during the holidays. So, don't feel like you're alone in that, by being away from family this year."

That was as understanding as could be. She couldn't get upset by that.

But she did. Her eyes went glassy, and she pushed the spoon around in the thick soup she'd ordered, like a plow, and watched the track fill back in behind the temporary path.

"I appear more out of practice than I thought." The only way to end this was just to cut to the chase, get it out so neither of them felt obligated to keep talking. "Yesterday was a bad day. I was incorrect to put you in the position I did. How do I correct this?"

She stopped her soup-plowing and lifted cautious eyes to him. Cautious but no longer clouded with the bitter cocktail of pain and anger there a moment before. The wariness wasn't exactly a great look, but it was better than his first attempt.

"That's all. To fix it, I mean. Thank you. I appreciate it. Yesterday was very difficult."

Today was a little better. "How are you doing with Conley?"

"Fine." She answered quickly, then spoke more easily. "She's very helpful. Kind. Welcoming. Got my locker fixed yesterday. Today hasn't been terribly busy, so I've mostly been learning the hospital's systems. Familiarizing myself with the layout of everything. Not so hands-on, but useful learning."

The lengthy answer didn't irritate him for once. He even found himself feeling more kindly to Conley for helping after he'd bungled the morning. This woman he didn't know at all somehow inspired something in him other than his own bitter cocktail of emotions that had been drugging his thoughts this year. Something that wasn't ugly and twisted. So, he kept talking in the hopes she'd stay and talk too.

"Important learning. If you like, you can shadow me the rest of the day. I tend to get anything interesting or difficult. I'm taking *shadow* to mean observe now. I'd just share thought process as I diagnose? Not tell you to diagnose."

Shadowing was probably supposed to be a teaching experience. And she wasn't a doctor, he had to remind himself again. She wasn't an emergency specialist, but they could both learn from those with another set of skills, if anything interesting came in.

He took a bite of his sandwich and feigned casual politeness, waiting for her answer.

It took her a year before she answered. "Can you just call me on the comm if you get something interesting? That way, I can still make sure I'm learning what I need to about operations, personnel and inventory in the meanwhile?"

"Sure." He agreed quickly. Too quickly. God, he had no idea how to talk to anyone anymore, let alone a caramel-haired beauty who'd managed to make him notice her as a woman, not just another possible source of danger.

CHAPTER FIVE

AFTER LUNCH, WHICH had carried on civilly once he'd apologized, Belle returned to the nurses' station and the binder of information she'd been given to digest.

Lyons had returned to prowling around Emergency as if he was taking a head-count. He was not the attending, he'd not been given charge of all the patients, but he looked into every single room—as spartanly packed as they happened to be—before he looked for his next case. Maybe he was looking to trade with another physician.

Or something else as odd as he was. What else was there to think about him?

Well, maybe she could say he was suffering from something too. That was the kinder description of *odd*. She was starting to wonder if he'd also suffered a loss.

Even that tiny tangential reference to Noelle made her eyes start to burn. She reached under the table to pinch her thigh sharply, drawing her mind back from paths she shouldn't take. Especially not at work. She had a task to focus on.

She flipped into the directory, where she could see and familiarize herself with the names of the different doctors and their departments.

There were a number of names in Emergency that she didn't recognize—those on a different shift.

There were italicized names, like Dr. Angel Conley,

whose specialty overlapped two departments. And there was the other McKeag. Wolfe. Both named for predatory animals. That wasn't messed up at all.

Wait. Were they twins?

Possibility. Something to ask Angel. Since she was dating Wolfe. And that would make her life even weirder, since she'd already pointed out how unpleasant Lyons could be.

And that Christmas was hard for *him*. Not hard for the McKeags. Whatever had happened seemed personal to Lyons.

Great. If she wasn't tumbling down her own deep, bleak rabbit hole, she was tumbling down his. And…had no idea what she'd just read in the binder of important information she'd been studying all morning. She flipped back a few pages to find the last words that had stuck with her before her attention rabbit-holed.

"Ysabelle Sabetta."

Her name erupted from the comm strapped to her chest, in a deep, sudden *Scottish* voice. She dropped the binder.

Hell.

How did she answer the thing?

She took a chance and pushed the green button while rising from her chair to fetch her binder. "Yes. Hi. This is Belle."

"Meet me at the east ambulance bay."

"Okay." She'd stuffed her head so full of information today she had to turn to the map posted on the wall to make sure she knew how to get to the east ambulance bay, but this was better than studying, even if it meant the possibility he might be setting her up to be judged again because she wasn't a doctor.

When she got there, Lyons was already waiting, and looking exceptionally vigilant.

"What's coming?"

"Neck injury." He turned slightly to look at her, but then

focused right back out of the sliding glass doors, arms folded across his chest.

His shoulders, wide and defined, made her want to ask if he worked out, but that was extremely creepy and inappropriate. Instead, she fell into a silent vigil beside him, as he got his brooding superhero glare on, watchful over the ambulance bay.

Neck injury?

Silence over. "What kind of injury?"

"Hit the steering wheel, didn't have on a belt. No airbags."

"Oh."

Whiplash? Broken neck? Tear to the carotid? She could come up with a lot of dangerous-sounding injuries.

Before she gave in to the urge to ask him *all the questions*, the ambulance rolled up and Lyons headed out into the blustery snow, coatless, and she felt compelled to follow, just to keep things civil and calm.

The paramedics gave a little more information, the vitals all seemed good, and the man's neck was braced, with him awake and alert.

They had him inside and heading for a predetermined room shortly, and Lyons began giving orders.

"Can someone tell me what we're doing?" the man asked, his voice grating so hard it almost carried a second tone.

She wasn't supposed to diagnose today, but she still wanted to help, and, as she was a nurse first, she knew something about that. "Sir, do you usually have a hoarse voice?"

"No," the man croaked.

Lyons nodded to her; she almost smiled. It might as well have been praise compared to all other interaction over patients.

"I'm going to take the brace off. I need you to be very still." Lyons unfastened the brace once Belle got her hands on the man's head to keep him from turning it.

Lyons looked up, met her gaze and there was the briefest second when he seemed to smile, and then he was focused on the patient again. Bigger praise. He *almost* smiled; the corners of his mouth twitched.

Stay focused on the patient, she reminded herself, *not on wondering what it would be like if Lyons smiled for real.* Better: What if he laughed?

"Swelling," she murmured, because that seemed the most dangerous thing to her right now and probably meant it was wrong—being the flashiest symptom and all. There was a nasty bruise in a slight bow across the front of his throat, but, still, the swelling could cut off air.

"Yes," Lyons answered her quietly, then asked the patient, "Do you feel any restriction to your breathing?"

"I don't know." If possible, he sounded worse.

"Hold him." It was said very quietly, just to her, but as she was already holding the man's head still she gathered how much pain Lyons expected to shortly induce.

The next warning was for the patient, then Lyons began to explore the swelling tissue with light pressure.

The first prod and the man went stiff, hands twisting in the blanket draped over him, all color draining from his face. But the symptom that really stood out: his neck made a strange, almost growling sound where Lyons pressed.

Two presses, and Lyons pulled his hands back.

The patient wasn't moving; she held his head still but couldn't not look at Lyons's face. The surprise she saw there mirrored her own.

"He's got a perforation in the larynx," Lyons announced, not prompting her for diagnosis this time, thank goodness, then grabbed the collar to put it right back on. As soon as he had it in place, but before he fastened the straps, he looked at her. "Go check to see what trauma surgeons are free right now. Refer whoever you find here."

The directive had such a calm, level quality, at odds with the haste she saw in his eyes.

"On it."

And she was, because she'd spent the day familiarizing herself with personnel and protocol, and that wasn't information from the last three pages she hadn't absorbed.

"And look for a free OR."

"OR?" the man repeated, catching up as Lyons affixed the straps.

"You need surgery right now, sir. I'm sorry, and it's going to be all right, but you have air escaping into the tissue in your neck from a hole torn in your throat. That will get very infected if we don't get to it immediately."

"It's dangerous?"

"It's dangerous to leave it, but the surgery isn't that bad, as surgeries go."

That was the last she heard before she ran back down the hall to the station.

Within two minutes she'd found a surgeon and gotten a nurse busy claiming an OR. And because she hadn't filled out any of those forms here, and because Lyons didn't need her now—he had plenty of people coming to help him—she stayed to learn that too.

It was nearly twenty minutes before he found her again, this time in person, no comms to startle her.

"Hey," she greeted first, still feeling a kind of jittery, nervous and excited energy. "Have you seen that before?"

"Once," he admitted, shaking his head. "That's all it takes for it to cement in your memory. That sound when you press on the air pockets."

"Supercreepy," she filled in, and he actually laughed, something she could see he didn't do often. He was a handsome man by any standards, but there was an almost boyish quality to his smile that hit her right in the chest and made her want him to laugh again.

"Kind of like a tiny, angry animal," he ventured. Joking?

"Little angry bobcat."

"That sounds too cute."

"A tiny, furious bunny rabbit." She upped the cute factor, unable to help herself or the smile she felt on her face, especially when he laughed again.

"Fighting for his last carrot."

"Cliché." She waved a hand. "Tiny, furious bunnies feast on raw onion for fun."

He was still smiling. "So noted."

And it was then I realized I was flirting with the man who'd made me batty yesterday.

Sometimes Belle mentally composed her emails to Noelle during the day, when she wanted to remember something, but if Belle was superstitious, she'd have sworn Noelle had just fed that line to her psychically to point out how insane this whole situation had turned. It even sounded like her sister.

Maybe it was, but she knew one thing for sure: while the card hadn't made him have a good day, it had *helped*. It had made a difference in his outlook. He was joking with her, not growling or yelling.

Then the guilt hit. They were joking over someone's suffering.

"He'll be okay though?" she asked, needing to hear it.

"He'll be okay. And I think in the future he'll wear his seat belt."

"Lucky to have a survivable life lesson."

His comm sounded again and he answered but nodded a farewell before heading off in another direction.

She needed a good gift to bring him Monday, and she had a whole weekend to shop for gifts and get pictures for Noelle.

Did people still come to New York to go shopping? Was that a thing? Two deeds, one stop. Noelle would like a picture of some iconic department stores.

Monday morning, Lyons arrived his customary hour early to his shift, and this time he knew the instant he entered the locker room he was alone. No stumbling over her. No morning chatting, not that he had anything to say, but she always seemed to when she wasn't panicking over something.

A mild sense of disappointment stymied him and quickened his steps. He had things to do, he didn't come in early to chat anyone up.

He'd spent the weekend convincing himself that the strange emotion that had overtaken him the past few days was to do with Christmas's rapid approach. And that was part of it. A sad anniversary he didn't want to note the passing of but which was marked in such a way that he'd never be able to forget. Not while living in a country that celebrated the holiday.

Maybe he just couldn't get past it as long as he worked Emergency—a thought that came to mind more often than he'd like. That he should quit. Move to the country. Buy a horse farm. Abandon…everyone—not that he was much use to the world as anything but a doctor, and he didn't want to continue that unfortunate McKeag tradition: living on the money, giving nothing back to the world.

Stepping to his locker, he unlocked it and his heel bumped something under the bench placed before it.

His stomach churned.

The object had moved when he'd bumped it and produced the sound of crinkling paper.

He carefully inched his feet forward.

It's nothing. Not another gift.

Locker open, he shed his coat and stowed everything. He took his time getting his stuff ready, and even paused to drain the coffee he'd walked in with—the coffee he'd bought with the card Conley had denied giving him on Friday when he'd confronted her with a cup of her own. Ignore it.

When the cup was empty, he walked to the trash and threw it in. He could've kept walking, not looking back to see what it had been, and hoping someone else would take care of it, but that idea irritated him almost as much as what he expected to see.

Enough.

He looked back, using the distance to see what his feet had touched.

Small box. Red paper. Green bow.

In front of his locker.

"Dammit."

It looked wrong somehow, but then everything did in red and green to his eyes now. Anything that reminded him of that day could trigger it, and those two colors especially. If someone had ever told him a color combination could ever have a malicious feel to them, he'd have assumed they were far too fixated on a sporting team and told them to get help. Instead, he saw the red and green box and thought it might be a trap of some sort. As if he might touch it and blow a hole in the hospital.

Beyond ridiculous. His foot had already hit it. If it had been wired to trigger by touch, he'd already be in pieces. This kind of thinking was the same as when he'd thought the subway had been tampered with. Nonsense. Paranoia. Ridiculous. Hard to dismiss or control. Infuriating.

And eating into his preparation time.

Storming back, he snatched the gift off the floor, saw his name neatly printed on a label—no handwriting for him to analyze—and ripped it open to reveal a book.

A humorous book about why Christmas sucked.

Which just proved that this was some kind of sick joke. Whoever was leaving the gifts knew he had trouble with Christmas—probably knew why, that his colleague had been murdered because he was sloppy—and was forcing this on him as punishment. This gift was notice: the truth of why he'd come to Sutcliffe was out after all they'd done to keep it quiet. He hadn't told anyone. Wolfe? Conley?

Or maybe he was losing his mind and should double-check before giving in to that reaction.

Grabbing his phone, he pressed the first of very few numbers he kept in the memory, and as soon as his brother answered, Lyons asked, "Are you giving me gifts?"

"Good morning." Wolfe's easy greeting went right along with his complete inability to take anything seriously. Well, anything but Conley, apparently, and his practice. "I haven't decided. Do you have something on your Christmas list?"

"Not *for* Christmas," he bit out. He should've known the conversation would go this way. "Now. I want to know if you're leaving gifts for me in the locker room. Now. Today."

He paused, only for a second, and when he spoke, sounded more serious. "Angel said you had brought her coffee and asked about a gift card. I didn't leave it."

"And a book this morning."

"Really?" He sounded far more interested suddenly. "No signature?"

"No writing. Printed label." He heard something and stopped, then walked to where he could see around the bank of lockers. No one. His ears were playing tricks. "And it's a book called *An A to Z Reference of Why Christmas Sucks*."

"Well, whoever sent it certainly knows you," Wolfe muttered. "Which leaves me out. And which I'm determined to change. You should come to dinner on Friday."

"Not this again."

"I'm going to keep asking until you say yes."

"I don't want to come to dinner, you know me enough to know that." He prowled back to his locker, and almost put the book inside, but the idea of corrupting the space set his teeth on edge. "Was it Conley? You told her about why I came to Sutcliffe, didn't you?"

"It wasn't Angel." Wolfe said her name pointedly, which assured Lyons would keep calling her by her surname. "I did tell her—we're doing this thing where we don't have secrets."

"Mistake."

Wolfe ignored his interruption. "But she isn't a gossip.

She hasn't told anyone, though I don't know why you want it to be a secret."

"Because I want Sutcliffe to be free of it. If people knew, they'd want to talk to me about it. I don't want them to talk to me."

And he didn't want pity. Or blame. Or reminders. He didn't need any of those.

And he didn't want people saying, *Oh, that's why he's such an ass.*

He had no interest in excuses. He was an ass because he was busy keeping everyone safe.

He came to work early so he could take inventory of the patients and keep an eye on anyone who might become a danger.

He poked his nose into all the rooms several times per day because he wanted to know who was there and who might harm his peers and other patients.

"Have you asked her if she's doing this?"

"I haven't. She told me the conversation you had and was as surprised that you seem to have an admirer as I was. She works with you, so she was probably the most surprised."

"Funny."

"Truthful."

"Well, ask her. If I have to ask her she'll like me even less, and might hold it against you."

"She wouldn't," Wolfe said, and in that instant Lyons could hear the first sounds of irritation in his brother's voice. "But I'll ask her directly. Don't go being a jerk to her just because she's dating me. She's suffering enough."

"Doesn't seem like she's suffering. She's having a ball playing Christmas elf with you."

Wolfe took the subject change and reverted to form. "I told her she'd better bring that little green outfit home for a good game of Santa's Naughty Little Mistress, but she said—"

Lyons hung up before his brother could finish. Mostly

because as he'd spoken, Lyons had started to imagine Sabetta in a little green elf outfit.

It had been a thong.

With a tiny bra.

And little pointy, curly-toed shoes, which should be the disturbing part, but wasn't. His body's quickening was the disturbing part.

But one glance at the book still in his hand and the mood left him. He slammed his locker shut and left, book in hand. He had to get to Lost and Found to make a deposit, then take his morning lap before his shift started. He didn't have time or desire for his body to indulge in such a...disturbance.

Lyons's whole day had held the tone set by that stupid book this morning.

He'd been vomited on and had to change.

He'd been chewed out by a cantankerous nonagenarian with a heart condition who was, "Just fine, thank you very much," even though her heart rate was around one hundred and sixty beats per minute and her blood pressure made him marvel that she'd not already had a stroke.

Finally, he'd missed the arrival of the addict who got violently angry over being given Narcan to save his life and ruin his high and tried to punch a nurse. Ineffectively, at least, but they'd been fortunate enough that the police had accompanied that patient and restrained him before he actually hurt anyone. They hadn't been able to stop for help before every patient was alarmed, and probably half the hospital.

He'd needed a cup after that and was slightly mollified to find that he'd left the gift card in his locker and purchased it himself.

He'd just stepped through the doors into the department when his comm fired, summoning him to the east ambulance bay.

He caught up with Sabetta in the east hallway, jogging

in the same direction, pulling on gloves. "Do you know what's coming?"

"Shooting. Robbery. A couple, I don't know if this is the shooter or victim," she answered, and although he knew his feet kept going, he didn't feel it. Not a single step vibrated up his legs. He could've been floating, except for the way his vision bounced.

She might have said something else, all sound seemed to come from a long way away—muffled and garbled, like words shouted into a glass jar. Soon enough, they were at the ambulance bay, and the blaring siren finally cut through.

Gunshot. Gunshot. He never took them, hadn't since his own shooting. Someone had always been around to handle these situations, or they went straight to the trauma surgeons. But today they'd called for *him* on the comm. There was no avoiding it. There was no one else.

The first ambulance stopped in the bay and the paramedics got out to help with the gurney.

They weren't supposed to ask the identity of the patient, but the fact that there was no cop in the ambulance with the woman said that she was a victim. He could think. He could do this. Help her.

Sabetta took over holding the compression bandage, and they all ran into the hospital for the trauma room.

"How many shots?" he asked, not wanting to lift the compress until they got her into the trauma room.

"Looks like one, but she's losing more blood than is coming out. We were there and as soon as he shot her the police moved in, so we got her here quickly," the paramedic replied, carrying the bag of saline he'd hung, "but her pressure is falling fast. It's only up enough now to function because of the saline."

First: stabilize her, preferably enough to wait on surgery. God help him, where were the trauma surgeons?

They got into the room and he shoved his hands into gloves, his hands shaking but manageable.

"Get her typed and hang blood. Now." He barked at the nearest RN. "Do we know who she is? Get her record."

He lifted the bandage to look and blood rushed out.

"It's not clotting at all, is it?" Sabetta said, her voice trembling just a little—this affected her too, but he couldn't try to take care of her now. Not and keep his mind together and help his patient.

"Get a PT/INR. There's a machine in the cabinet." No need for a finger-stick, there was plenty of blood.

He heard the cabinets opening as he used his free hand to squeeze the saline bag to pump a little more into her veins, though the blood already looked thin. Might be too thin to test for the presence of anticoagulants.

It was too much blood. Bullets liked to ricochet around inside bodies, bouncing off bones and shredding organs. Organs bled. And then people died.

He couldn't put it off, hoping for a trauma surgeon to show up, he had to open now and find the source of the bleeding.

"Drape her and get an anesthetist here now."

He pressed Sabetta's hand to the quarter-sized hole in the woman's side. "Compress."

She nodded and swapped in some fresh gauze to pack the wound, leaving him to poke his head out of the trauma room and shout for more hands.

Within five minutes, they had hung blood, brought in several extra units on standby and transformed the trauma room into a makeshift surgical suite. It was equipped for this kind of emergency, but he hadn't had to use it for this since he'd come to Sutcliffe.

There was nothing to do but shut it down, look at the task as a physical puzzle. It was a projectile, not a bullet.

He cut down from the hole on her side, and the sheer amount of shredded tissue almost flattened him.

Big bullets didn't just slice through flesh, they caused crushing damage like a body hit by a high-speed train.

He'd been luckier. His bullets had been small caliber. They hadn't had the power or angles needed to bounce around and cause damage. They'd passed through his chest, missing vital areas, through his shoulder…and out the back. Hers had ricocheted off one rib, splintering it, then ripped through her spine as the new shards of rib left damage tracks of their own.

The left pulmonary artery was shredded, and he could see how little blood now reached the lungs by the color the tissue had turned. The left lung was pale. Gray. Dead.

He did what he could to patch the artery. That was the primary source of the major blood loss. If he could stop that, he might be able to stabilize her. Then the surgeons could make the repairs to her body over the course of a few days, giving her time to heal in between.

"She's getting cold," Sabetta said. He'd been feeling the same, but so focused, trying to hurry. He couldn't let her get too cold.

Even if she was alive, her blood wouldn't be able to clot if her body temperature fell too low. At a certain point, there would be no hope.

"Get her temp."

"Ninety-two."

"Put a heating blanket over her legs. Set it as high as it will go."

He found two other blood vessels that had been damaged, one on the surface of the heart, well beyond his experience level. He needed a trauma surgeon. Or a cardiac surgeon. Or a thoracic surgeon. Or just a damned surgeon. Instead, she had him. And he stitched the great cardiac vein? Left circumflex artery? God, he couldn't tell which one it was in the damage, but he stitched.

While he worked, he heard his team doing as directed, but it wasn't working. She was getting colder.

"Ninety," Sabetta announced, and though he doubted

she'd ever participated in a single surgery, every time he asked for anything, she provided.

It took less than an hour for the patient's temperature to drop past all effort to save her. He knew before he closed that she wouldn't clot. That pulmonary artery was still oozing, and it was the first he'd repaired. Same for the one on the surface of her heart.

Even the holes made by his stitches continued to ooze blood.

It wasn't going to work. Even if she'd been on anticoagulants, they'd given her sufficient fresh, un-medicated blood to put her blood back into a clotting range. It was her temperature. They just couldn't get her warm.

Before he closed, her heart stopped beating. It gave a couple of convulsive beats, then just quit. There would be no restarting it, he knew, but tried to massage the battered organ with his hands anyway.

Nothing. Adrenalin didn't help. Nothing they tried helped.

"Lyons?"

It was Ysabelle's soft voice at his ear that stilled him.

"You need to call it."

She was right. He knew she was right, but it took her gloved, bloody hand on his to get through.

It hadn't been like this when he'd been shot. He'd stayed awake for most of it. Felt the hot bolts of pain from the impacts, then from his friends picking him up from the blood-soaked floor to move to a stretcher. He'd seen the gray, grim faces, peering down at him, watched them pause and then lie when he'd asked about Eleni.

He'd had Wolfe transfer him to another facility as soon as he'd been able, unable to look at them afterward. Then cut them out of his life. He should probably at least tell them he was okay now, but it would be a lie.

He made the call and stepped back so the team could take

care of her, mentally going over the protocol, the things he was supposed to do. "I need to see if there's family."

"Not like that," Sabetta said, directing his gaze down to the fresh scrubs he'd just changed into, now shiny and slick with so much blood it could only make the black material red by volume.

She urged him out of the trauma room, and didn't stop until she'd steered him into the office he liked to hole up in. "Do you have a change of scrubs in your office?"

"My office?" Her words didn't make any sense.

"This isn't your office?"

"Communal…"

"Oh." She pulled the gloves off and threw them into the trash, then began to rifle through a cabinet.

CHAPTER SIX

THE OFFICE CABINETS had nothing to help Belle deal with an obviously shell-shocked and blood-covered Lyons.

Gunshot victims had been the main situation for her to fear since she'd entered emergency medicine. If she was honest, that was probably a factor in her decision to always work at small facilities and Urgent Cares. Places that were unlikely to see a critical gunshot victim.

But that decision had been made for her when she'd been unable to find such a position in New York during the time she needed.

There had been a tight ball of panic in her chest through the whole struggle to help their patient, even without the weight of it on her shoulders as it had been on Lyons's shoulders.

She looked back at him and found him in exactly the same position she'd left him. He said nothing. His eyes were open, but he might not even be seeing her, as unfocused as they looked. He was naturally fair skinned, but now had a pallor rivaling the dead.

Goodness, he couldn't go talk to the family. Not like this.

"Lyons?" She used his first name, and it got a reaction. He looked at her, or toward her. He'd held it together for the emergency surgery, but at that second, he was just gone. Retreated into himself.

Sweet heaven, what had happened to him?

She needed to get him changed. And herself. "Sit here."

It took very little for her to ease him onto the edge of the laminate desktop, and only a second to flick up the tag at the back of his scrub top to see the size. They had spare scrubs available to staff; she'd seen them when Angel had given her the department tour. She just needed badges...

Looking down, she spied his hanging from the pocket of his scrub bottoms, snatched it up and said, "Stay here. I'll be right back."

It didn't look as if he was going anywhere. He stared at the wall, didn't acknowledge her words or anything, and if her heart hadn't been in her throat before, now it felt clogged.

She darted out of the office and ran for the staff room, and the scrubs machine.

A couple of minutes later, she'd checked out scrubs for her and for him, grabbed a package of wet wipes and ran back to the office to find him there still.

"Lyons?" She tried to say his name with the kind of steady strength she'd hoped would comfort him, but her voice disobeyed. It wobbled. Sounded pained. Scared.

She tugged her own bloody top off and reached for the hem of his shirt and had it half up when he caught her wrists.

Sitting on the edge of the desk put the tall Scot at eye level with her, and he came back into focus staring into her eyes. Despite the blood and the trauma, there was an intimate pull in the locked gaze. Not sexy, it wasn't even like that, but connected. A connection strong enough that it strengthened her in return.

"Ysabelle?" He said her name back, scowl returning as he pushed past the parts of himself that had been shredded.

"There you are." She kept her voice soft, gentle. "We're changing, okay?"

"Your top is gone."

"I was going to get you cleaned off before I put on my own clean top."

He looked down, noted her ruined bra and the dried blood still on her arms and torso, and focused. "I can do it. You… Do you have…?"

She gestured to the big package of wet wipes. "Enough to get most of it until a shower is possible."

He nodded—apparently, she'd inferred the right question he'd been stumbling through—and pulled off both his tops. "Clean up. Take off that bra."

He turned his back to her, and to give him some semblance of privacy, she turned her back too. Using the wet wipes, she cleaned her face—certain there'd been some blood on her forehead—then worked her way down. Neck. Shoulders. Then pulled off her bra, cleaned her chest and arms, and slipped her fresh top on.

They'd not had time to gown. They'd not had time for anything.

When she turned back around, he was dressed, but stood with his hands on the surface of the desktop, bent, as if he couldn't support his own weight well enough to stand up.

He was better now than he had been immediately afterward, but this was not a man who could go speak to the patient's family.

Would anyone else do it?

"Sit," she urged again, but this time steered him to a chair. The man, while far larger than she, was unnaturally pliant.

When he was seated, still looking pale and dazed, the decision was made for her. She couldn't let him go out there; it wouldn't be a comfort to the family, and he might collapse under the weight of it.

She didn't want to do it, had never done this particular duty. She'd been present when bad news was given, but never death.

Which was why when she'd wanted to come to New York, she should've held out for an Urgent Care position. She wasn't equipped to deal with death talks. She wasn't even sure she was equipped to deal with Lyons or help in any way that mattered.

But she could share the load for today.

Before she could lose her nerve or talk herself out of it, she said to his barely cognizant face, "You stay. I'm going to go talk to the family."

And then she stepped out. *Just go do it. Don't cry. Say they did all they could.* Say she was sorry. Offer to listen. Answer questions. Lie. Lie and say the surgeon had been pulled into another emergency surgery, but that she had assisted. She could answer their questions. Just keep Lyons out of it; he wasn't up for this conversation.

A chaplain. She should bring a chaplain with her.

Calling on the comm took a few minutes, but when the gentle-looking woman joined her, she went out in search of the family.

Over the next quarter-hour, she explained to a grieving husband and son that the woman they called wife and mother would not be returning to them. That they'd done all they could. That the bullet had struck her heart. How sorry she was.

All the same things she'd been told when her father had been shot. Maybe even in the same order, but she didn't say, *Wrong place, wrong time.* That didn't help. Never helped.

She must have cried, because the chaplain looked worriedly at her a time or two. She didn't know. All she did know was she was glad to have changed and cleaned up. They were suffering enough without seeing the amount of blood that had sprayed from a loved one. No one needed that memory.

Lyons sat in the office chair, staring up at the ceiling, mentally listing every breed of horse he could remember, along with the names of any mounts he'd ridden of those breeds. He couldn't say when it had become a way to try and exert control, take back his mind when the memories of that day took control. Prevent what came next: examining everything he'd done, thinking of all the things he could've done, what might've changed it.

"Lyons? Lyons."

He pulled his gaze from the ceiling and focused on her concerned face. When had she come back? How had he missed her, standing right over him?

"What?"

He should probably go home. He was no use to anyone here, and the day was almost done. Or maybe it was done.

"I said put your head down. You're breathing too fast." As she spoke, her hand settled against his cheek, warm and alive, delicate but with strength there that he did not feel in that moment. Better than listing horses—when she touched him, every thought drifted away. Peace flowed through her touch, like a drug.

He tilted his head into the touch, but she shifted her hand to the back of his neck and, leaning in, voice coaxing, said again, "You're breathing too fast."

He was? He didn't notice, but if it meant she'd keep touching him, he'd do whatever she asked.

She crouched to follow him down, and soon was on knee level with him, hand still warm on the back of the neck.

"Breathe like me," she said, her breath fanning the side of his head, and lifted one of his hands to her chest to feel the rise and fall, the cadence of her breathing.

He felt the difference then and heard it—with her cheek pressed against his head, mouth close to his ear. She breathed far slower than he was. She was right, he had to slow down…

"Hold." She spoke, trying to help. "Breathe."

No one outside their little huddle could've heard, and in that intimate embrace he wanted to obey but his body had other ideas, still convinced he needed more air.

"Hold," she said again, catching him on the third breath, and this time when she directed him, her hand began to knead the back of his neck, and the muscles he knew were corded and tight. When they started to give, it was like a waterfall; the release spread through his shoulders and down over his back, and he relaxed into her, his breath slowing with it.

Her touch was magic, or maybe it was just her proximity. She wrapped his hand in hers and her thumb stroked back and forth across the back of his hand, slow and rhythmic, and he found his breath slowing to the time she set.

Over the years, he'd been told by many—mostly nurses—that touch healed, and he'd scoffed. Stupid.

The spike of adrenalin, which he could now identify, passed and everything got a little easier. Thinking. Not thinking. Taking the peace that flowed from her hands and cheek against his head.

When he breathed slowly enough for her to be satisfied, she leaned back. The loss of her made him look up to fill the distance growing between them. That fog wasn't gone; he felt it still around the edges, pressing in.

Not ready. Not yet.

He stood, pulling her to her feet with him so he could get his arms fully around her. Even if it was selfish of him to take what she offered, she slid her arms around his torso in response and laid her cheek against his shoulder.

They stood that way for some time, his chin resting on her forehead, breathing in concert.

He could've stayed like that for hours, and certainly stayed that way longer than he should've, but couldn't make himself care. He'd stick right there until she put him away from her.

"Who did you lose?" Her question came and, although he didn't want to break the spell, her hands petting up and down his back soothed it out of him.

"She wasn't mine."

Lyons took pains to never talk about that day. Wolfe had

tried a little at first, and with more vigor lately, but Lyons could have lived his whole life fighting that talk.

But now… With everything that had gone on today, with this woman who was practically a stranger, he wanted to answer.

"She wasn't mine," he said again, marveling at how easy it came. "But I couldn't save her."

"She was your friend?" she asked, still holding tight.

"Yes." He didn't know how else to answer. The situation had involved someone else's marriage, usually forbidden territory to him. He minded his own business. His parents had their fill of affairs and he'd witnessed the carnage that spiraled out of them, but with her, he'd broken his own rules in the name of helping. But he'd only made it worse.

"You loved her."

"No." Love didn't enter into it and he didn't know if that made his guilt better or worse. One thing he did know: this kind woman wouldn't offer her comfort so freely if she knew Eleni's death was on his hands. And it was.

"When?"

"Christmas Eve," he answered, a little amazed that the answers kept coming. He didn't have to tell the story this way; she prompted, and he answered. It came easier.

"Oh, Lyons, I'm so sorry."

"Don't do that," he rasped. He didn't want her sympathy, didn't deserve it. He might be able to accept the comfort of her touch, but he couldn't accept her emotional investment in him. He couldn't accept sympathy.

Before she truly pitied him, he added, "I'd appreciate if you didn't tell anyone. I don't like people to know."

Even if he hadn't told her half of it—he hadn't told her he'd been shot in the process, or that it had happened at work. And he wouldn't, or she'd really pity him, or refuse to accept the truth of his guilt in it.

Her arms relaxed just a little, and his instinctively tightened, still not ready. The extra squeeze made her tremble, or was he just getting out of his own head enough to notice?

He stilled, and it continued—light, but there. Not fleeting. Constant.

"You're trembling."

"I know… I'm sorry."

He held tighter again but forced his arms to relax before he crushed her. "Don't apologize. Is it me?"

Or the shooting? Or talking to the family?

Breaking bad news was never easy, but for all he knew, this was her first time—and no one should perform that duty for the first time alone. If she had, she'd done it for him. And he'd let her.

That would make this worse—not just because he took the comfort she offered but took it when she needed it herself.

"Who did you lose?" he asked, hoping that was the reason, like a true bastard who didn't want even another drop of guilt pressing him down.

"My dad," she replied, just as he had done. Quiet words that belied the damage they caused.

He closed his eyes. Wrong again. And the only thing that would be worse than him hoping her pain wasn't his fault would be to leave her alone with it now.

"How?"

"Line of duty," she whispered, both sliding quieter and quieter, as if the words themselves were dangerous.

She'd lost her dad in the line of duty.

"Cop?"

She nodded.

He'd been shot. Dammit.

"When?" His voice went hoarse and she pulled back to look up at him, though she stayed within the circle of his arms. Her dark eyes searching his. Still trying to make sure *he* was all right.

He wasn't all right.

"When?" he repeated, giving her a little jostle. If he had a drop of strength left in him, he'd shake it out of her.

"I was fourteen," she said, and then she was peeling her arms away.

Still not ready to let go.

His hands went to the back of her head and pulled her back to him, anything to keep her there with him, and he suddenly didn't care if she hugged back because he needed it and she realized that, or because she needed it too. Even if it couldn't wind back the clock and keep her from doing what had hurt her to do.

"Why didn't you tell me?"

"You needed me to do it."

She might not have meant it to, but the soft words carved into his pride.

He couldn't think of a single bad thing she'd done in their short acquaintance. She'd been scared of him at first, but even despite having seen him at his surliest, she was still kind to him when he needed it. God help him, he might be holding a genuinely good person in his arms, or his own private angel.

He leaned back, not letting go, but needing to see her. She tilted her head back to look up at him, her eyes damp and redness there he couldn't believe he'd missed before.

She did need comfort. When her gaze tracked briefly to his mouth, instinct took over.

Before he knew it, he'd angled his head to her mouth, and she leaned up on her toes to meet him.

The sweet, warm heat of her lips threw his heart into an unruly rhythm, and heady, intoxicating tingles spread from his lips down over his chest, reaching all the way to the hand he'd threaded into her caramel-hued tresses.

She'd met him; she needed this too. He clutched her to him, holding tightly enough to nearly lift her from her feet, just because he needed closer. Deeper.

The bitter grief that had dragged them together faded in the tide of something honeyed, something glowing.

She clung to him, and before he knew it, they'd moved onto the desktop—he'd laid her out and followed her down.

Since the shooting, he'd distanced himself from everyone. There had been no sweetness in his life; he hadn't let there be. He hadn't wanted it. But in that moment, he would've said or done anything to get closer to her, and it salved his pride to know it gave back something he'd taken from her.

Belle clutched at his back, wrapped and reveling in the solid bulk of him. In his heat. She didn't know why he was kissing *her*, or why she was kissing him back, aside from simply wanting to.

Everything she'd seen about him, from his quick temper to cradling and massaging the heart of a patient with tears in his eyes, to the devastation that clung to him when he lost her, all said he'd suffered and deserved kindness, tenderness. His kiss said he needed to be touched, that he craved the kind of affection his actions likely kept at bay.

Something more than attraction had her clawing at his back to get closer. It might have been built on making him into a repository for her Christmas needs, or a desire to have someone meaningful in her life or *to be* that to someone else, or maybe it was just an instinctive answering call to his own need.

She didn't know or care. She just wanted more of this.

Her hands tangled in his hair and she slid one leg up to hook over him as his heat pressed her into the cold desk surface and shifted so that had there been no clothing in the way, everything would've gotten far more serious.

Another shift, this time from him, and the cotton scrub bottoms felt like nothing at all. Neither did her top. His hand found her breast, and her bra gone, and he groaned into her mouth as his thumb began a rhythmic stroke over the peaked nipple.

A loud noise jolted him back, and both heads jerked to the door, expecting to find someone there, caught. But there was no one.

He still lay against her, and his breathing, fast and heated, fanned her cheek as those pale blue eyes fixed on hers. "Telephone."

"Huh?"

"We knocked off the telephone."

Mundane words, almost emotionless despite the breathlessness that buoyed them, but the set of his brows and the way he looked back and forth from her eyes to her mouth said he was trying to decide whether he should kiss her again, but wanted to.

She made the decision for him, tugging his head back to hers. She wanted to stay there, drift in his kisses a little longer. When his tongue slipped into her mouth, she forgot to question why she was doing it. There was no reason not to, at least not that she could recall. His arm, beneath her shoulders, cradled her head from the hard surface of the desk, and his other hand returned to her breast, his long elegant fingers cupping, massaging, stroking...

He knew how to kiss, how to touch, and only when she'd frantically begun pulling at the hem of his top, mindlessly wanting more, did he pull back.

Not only back, he slipped his arm from below her head, and stood to walk away from the desk, leaving her senses reeling.

His hands fell to his hips, and, facing the wall, back to her, he gulped air, leaving her to gather her own wits, or what was left of them.

"This is a mistake," he said roughly, and after another several deep, forcibly slow breaths turned to look at her.

She'd worried his hair, which he kept a little longer on the top than she normally liked, into a bit of a tangle.

"Why?" she asked, making herself sit up, and right her top. It probably was a mistake, but not for whatever reason he thought—unless he realized she was the one leaving him gifts.

Which suddenly felt kind of deceitful instead of in the spirit in which she'd intended.

If they'd leapfrogged over all other relationship activity and were at the point of *kissing* now, did that mean she needed to change her Secret Santa plan? Did it cross some kind of honesty line to keep it up? He'd enjoyed the gifts, she thought. Maybe. Or maybe hadn't been bothered one way or another. Friday he'd been in a good mood, but today was her second gift, and he'd been in a bad one—even before the shooting victims had come in, he'd prowled around the department, biting the head off anyone who'd looked at him wrong. Statistically, it was a wash, no way to tell one way or the other. Unless she asked him, but that would give her away entirely.

He said something about the end of shift having passed, picked up the telephone they'd knocked to the floor, said goodnight and then just left her sitting there, a little stymied about what had happened and why.

He'd said mistake, but nothing in his kiss had echoed the sentiment. The only part of her questioning her decisions was aimed at the gifts right now.

Slowly, she slid from the desk and straightened her clothes. The bloody scrubs they'd discarded had been forgotten, and she couldn't blame him. He hadn't been right since their patient had arrived, and that was the only reason she should reconsider kissing him again in the future. All this might have been her taking advantage of him. Except that he'd kissed her first. No, at the worst, it was the two of them seeking some kind of comfort.

Nanna had been right: Those who hurt others were suffering too.

Lyons had been hurt, he'd lost someone and blamed himself. *I couldn't save her.*

If they were going to continue exploring this attraction, she'd have to stop the gifts, for sure.

But not now. He wasn't continuing this exploration, or the kisses, so she had no reason to stop either.

He needed kindness and care, and she needed someone to give to.

CHAPTER SEVEN

THE NEXT MORNING was busy, and Belle only caught sight of Lyons once as she was heading into the room of a patient.

After his departure, she'd done everything she could to avoid thinking about the forbidden office, including an hour of man-shopping on a dating site, and being excessively uninspired to even put anything in her cart.

They'd passed in an empty hallway, and he'd looked long enough that she'd known he'd seen her before he'd looked away. Not approaching. Not even nodding hello. It was next-level snubbing. Snubbing with purpose. Which pretty much cleared up the question of whether or not they were going to be doing more kissing in the near future.

And stung more than she'd like.

The last thing Belle needed was a relationship, hence the aborted man-shopping. What she wanted was friends. Casual friends. Friends she wouldn't grow too attached to. Not someone else she'd spend the rest of her life mourning when she inevitably lost them.

Leaving the cafeteria cashier with her tray, she spotted a likely friend candidate she hoped to not get too attached to: Dr. Conley, sitting alone, with a book, at the small table off to the side of the cafeteria where Belle also liked to seclude herself.

Angel, as she'd insisted Belle call her, had been kind to her from day one, and even had warned her about Lyons's difficulty with Christmas, so that made her the perfect friend she wouldn't get too attached to: someone who might be an ear and give the advice she couldn't get from Noelle, but who was already attached to Lyons's brother so would have to go only one direction if some kind of skirmish did break out between her and the wounded doctor.

She headed over.

"Hi, do you mind if I join you?" she asked, and, when Angel looked up, nodded to the book. "I can choose another table if you're engrossed in reading. I personally hate it when I'm in a book and someone interrupts…"

"Oh, I'm not that engrossed, sadly. It's supposed to be a suspense, but the author keeps telescoping the punches, so I've seen all of them coming. I'm mostly reading now out of spite, and the hope that she surprises me somehow."

Belle laughed despite herself and settled down opposite Angel. "I know that feeling. Usually happens when a book has been massively hyped to me and then it's Disappointment City."

"That's actually the sixth borough of New York: Disappointment City. Populated with out-of-work actors, aging chorus girls and people who believed the hype…"

Angel's joking helped relieve the worry that had haunted her since she'd placed Lyons's gift this morning: a box of Scottish tablet she'd made because she honestly had no idea what to get the man even now, but figured all bachelors appreciated homemade food and the internet said this was a traditional Scottish treat. And even if she wasn't sure she'd done it correctly it did taste good. And it looked like the pictures she'd found and was easier than fudge. Besides, the knitting she'd started on Saturday wasn't done.

But suddenly, the chuckle she'd shared turned into a spontaneous confession—what she was doing with the presents, not the kissing. Angel listened, fully present, but didn't look as if she quite understood. In a supportive way.

"He was mean to you, so you decided to kill him with kindness?" she asked, half grinning through her confusion.

"Not kill him. He needs kindness, and I don't have anyone to give presents to this year, so I thought maybe it was Secret Santa time."

"And you're changing your mind because of the way he's storming around?"

"I thought he was just storming at me."

"Why would he be just storming at you?" Angel asked a lot of questions but didn't sound judgmental.

The more they talked, the more comfortable it became.

It was on her lips to *really* confess, but she was saved by her mouth refusing the task.

"Shared attraction he doesn't want to share," she said instead.

That got Angel's attention. "Oh, really…"

"Not mutually *desired* attraction," Belle amended. "But now that this is a thing, I've been thinking it might be weird for me to keep giving him secret presents. But he likes them, right? You said he thanked you."

"I don't know if I'd say he likes them. I think he was trying to be polite to me because I'm living with his brother."

The other McKeag. The one who did Christmas Things with Angel and didn't yell at everyone.

"So, he doesn't like them?"

Angel put her sandwich down and went silent as she considered the answer to this. "I don't know. I think he needs kindness too. He's had a very hard time this past year."

"He said."

Angel's brows shot up again. "He told you?"

Belle nodded. "We had a shooting victim yesterday and he had…difficulty."

Talking about that seemed wrong, so Belle waved a hand to get past it. "If you think I should stop, I'll stop. I don't want to make matters worse. I'm sure I can find someone else to give presents to. Maybe I'll bake cookies for the break room and give to everyone."

Angel thought for a moment then said, "You should keep doing it. How many more are you going to do?"

"I was going to keep hitting the work days until he went off for the holiday."

"He's not going off for the holiday," Angel said. "He's working every day except Christmas Eve. He doesn't want to work on Christmas Eve."

The anniversary of the death of his friend.

"Understandable," she murmured.

"I guess, but I wish he'd come upstate with Wolfe and me. We've rented a nice country house a few hours north of the city. He refuses all invitations. Wolfe's starting to get a little desperate. He doesn't think we should leave him alone in the city, and I'm starting to agree. The closer Christmas comes, the more he's growling at people."

Belle frowned then; she hadn't put that together, didn't know him well enough to know that pattern.

"But he's talking to you about it?" Angel asked.

"I don't know if I would say that. I would say in a moment of need, I was there, and he spoke reflexively. He certainly has been avoiding me *today*. Not even a hello when he should've said hello."

"That's not about the gifts. He doesn't want people knowing what happened. It was a hospital in a different hospital system across the city, and shootings happen so frequently, it's hardly news anymore. Someone was shot, they may or may not say it on the news. They mentioned the shooting on one channel, but not the names of those involved, except the shooter who later killed himself. When Wolfe convinced Lyons to come to Sutcliffe to work, keeping it quiet was one of his conditions. It's probably good that he's talking to you, even if it's just reflexively. He never talks to anyone."

Maybe the gifts were helping. Maybe knowing someone

cared had worked in conjunction with yesterday's painful situation and allowed him to speak.

She ate for a while in silence and, before Angel got ready to go, asked, "So, what would you give him? I need ideas."

Lyons had never had a kiss haunt him. Not in his entire adult life.

He'd fondly remembered kisses, given them replays in his mind and looked forward to receiving more, but he'd never felt consumed. He'd never felt his lips buzz and heat or his mouth water just from remembering a kiss. He'd never lain awake, examining from every angle, looking for the reason for his fixation. Before now.

As he'd been doing every spare moment.

That was the reason he'd waited for her lunch to be nearly over before he hit the cafeteria and brought his lunch back to the small, communal office—avoidance. The cold-turkey method of fighting craving or addiction, which was what this had started feeling like. He'd read the literature on addiction; he knew people could become addicts with one experience with different drugs.

She had all the drugging aspects.

Highly pleasurable combined with the dangerous ability to transport him momentarily out of his miserable existence. That was what created addicts.

Add the sweetness, or the apparent sweetness, and this morning's gift—a box of home-made candy—and he couldn't imagine another person making it for him.

It had to be Ysabelle. He just didn't know why. And for that reason, he wasn't going to eat the stuff, even if just thinking about it made his mouth water and his stomach growl…like a furious bunny rabbit.

Lyons took the entire hour and, forty minutes later, emerged from the secluded office to go see what was on the board and do his usual head-count.

But there were so many heads. Sometime in the last

hour, the number of patients had exploded. Ninety percent of the faces he saw were men in sports jerseys, many with evidence of a brawl on their faces: black eyes, split lips, broken noses…

He grabbed Conley's elbow as she hurried past. "What's going on?"

"There you are." She shook her head, not even pretending to not be exasperated, "Local hockey tournament broke out in a brawl. They're all half lit, and we've divided the department into halves to keep them separated. Go find someone to see to."

Drunken hockey players?

Every single internal alarm bell rang in unison. Conley had all but said mayhem was about to break out in the department, and all this happened while he was on lunch?

Running on fury, he headed into the monitoring station to look at the charts.

Broken nose. Broken bones. Contusions. Lacerations to be stitched. Two with abdominal trauma who had been referred to trauma surgeons.

And they were loud. How could he keep an ear out for the sound of trouble when it all sounded like trouble?

He grabbed a possible broken-arm case and took a circuitous route to the patient's room, looking in all the rooms as he passed. He found the men and women on both sides of the department looking equally furious, along with the scent of beer and the occasional vomit.

Just beside his room, he saw Sabetta with an especially thick-necked man with a bloody head bandage, trying to get him onto the gurney. Beside the bed, she had a table laid out with stitching supplies.

"Mr. Corbin, you have to lie down so I can stitch up your head," she said, speaking gently to him, as if that was going to get through. She was too damned sweet for this.

He stopped in the doorway, making himself pause and

let her try to handle it despite every ounce of him wanting to jump in and stop this from going further.

It took effort, restraining his body when blood rushed in his ears and every muscle tensed, ready to spring.

She looked away from her patient, fixing her gaze on him standing in the doorway, and his morning's message of avoidance came back to bite him. She looked him dead in the eye and walked toward him and *shut the door*.

He was close enough he had to step backward to keep from being hit by the door.

Damn. Now what? How was he supposed to move on to another patient when drama was clearly brewing in there with her and the behemoth?

Conley passed by, brows up at him, a question he ignored. If Belle was going to have trouble, it'd be in the next few minutes, trying to get the man—

A loud clatter—the sound of something being thrown or knocked over—erupted inside and Lyons launched himself through the door.

She had her hands up, palms forward, warily circling with the drunk man, trying to be calm and coax him to the table.

That wouldn't work.

"Lie down and let the lady stitch your head," Lyons barked at the man, flinging the broken-arm file he'd been carrying onto the counter to free his hands, and stormed forward, making himself as broad and ready as possible.

"It's okay. He wants his head fixed, right, Mr. Corbin?" She was still trying, but upon Lyons's interference, her voice became more pleading than authoritative, and he couldn't say if it was because of him or the fight coming if the man took one more wrong step.

Corbin might be drunk and have a neck like a tree stump, but he was also clearly starting to sober up—at least enough to make the calculation that Lyons would lay him out if he didn't back down.

Lyons held the man's gaze, and, although his fist remained balled at his side, kept his voice level and *quiet*. "Settle down, or I'll sedate you so hard you'll be in adult diapers for a week."

Sometimes a calmly leveled threat worked better than shouted profanities, but Lyons was still thankful for the post-shooting therapy that started the gym routine that built the kind of strength and bulk to contain and intimidate a drunken hockey thug.

He didn't look at Belle, but, feeling her behind him, reached back to grasp her hip and guide her so that when he turned, allowing Corbin passage to the bed, she stayed behind him.

Corbin sat and then just lay down, but Lyons didn't leave her alone with the man. He moved to the uninjured side, allowing Belle access where she needed to stitch after she righted the tipped tray and gathered fresh supplies.

Then, with hands as steady as a surgeon, she exposed the wound, picked up the syringe to numb it, and set about stitching.

The broken arm he'd been going after could wait for however long it took. He wasn't leaving her to deal with this guy alone.

The vantage gave him a chance to observe her suture technique.

He worked Emergency and tended to go for the kinds of sutures that got the job done in the fastest space of time—simple, interrupted sutures. Sometimes simple running sutures. There were a few other techniques he knew, out of a veritable smorgasbord of stitching techniques, but this was one he did not know.

"What is that technique?"

"Running horizontal mattress suture." She said the words slowly, and then explained, "They're a bit more time-consuming, but they heal the best. Less scarring, which is good for a face wound."

"I'm going to look like Frankenstein," Corbin almost whined.

"Not if you're still," she muttered to the man, who actually hadn't moved since she'd begun. He also looked a little pale, as if he might be considering consequences finally, as the haze of alcohol started to clear.

"Where did you learn it?"

"I had a teacher who would take the time. I wanted to learn every stitch type. Practiced on chicken breasts from the grocery store."

He felt himself smiling, which would completely wreck his intimidating glare, and resumed watching the patient with a sobering stare.

"You have to be careful with tension," she explained. "If it puckers, it's a do-over because the tissue will be strangled, and the scar worsened."

"I'll be still," Corbin said, not even moving his mouth all that much when he spoke in case it should move his forehead.

Within ten minutes, she had him stitched and a nurse came in to bandage the wound. Although he'd not acted back-up, they both stayed until she was done. Lyons left the room with Belle and followed close until she stopped to look at him.

"Did he hurt you?"

She looked down at her upper arm, and half shrugged. "It's probably going to bruise, but it's not the end of the world."

He'd put his hands on her.

Lyons looked back down the hall toward the room they'd just left.

"Stop." She said one word, interrupting his consideration of violent acts against the patient, then added, "Thank you for coming to help me."

Dismissed? She resumed walking back down the hallway, leaving him there.

He still felt that connection to her, strongly enough to know that his rebuffing earlier—along with her own right now—smarted for them both.

"You did good work in there. I told you that you can ask if you need anything. That still goes." He caught up with her easily and took her hand to give a little squeeze. It was the most he could do. If they were alone, he'd have hugged her, probably kissed her again. Thank God they weren't alone. He already felt eyes on them.

"Thank you," she said again and didn't squeeze his hand in return, but she did stop walking, and looked down to where he still held her hand. A pointed reminder.

He let go, hadn't really meant to keep holding it, just stop her for a moment, make some kind of connection, smooth over the roughness he felt between them.

"I need to update the file." She nodded over his shoulder, still obviously upset with him.

And that was probably for the best. Letting attraction run amok would just lead them both down dangerous paths.

He had his own patient. Possible broken arm. He needed to see to that.

CHAPTER EIGHT

"HEY, BELLE?" ANGEL'S voice came from behind Belle as she stood at the computer, recording patient data.

The tinge of apprehension in Angel's voice made her turn. "Everything okay?"

"Wolfe's in the break room, came for a visit and asked if you had time for coffee?"

Lyons's brother wanted to meet her?

"Sure, I just need to enter the diagnosis and sign discharge and I'll be right there."

Angel smiled, looking relieved, as if she'd crossed some kind of "new friend" line in inviting her to coffee. Which meant Wolfe was there to see her because of *Lyons*, not to meet his girlfriend's new friend.

Which was fine. She knew better than anyone how different siblings could be, but she still wanted to meet the man who'd grown up with Lyons.

When she stepped into the break room to find only the two of them, standing in a warm embrace, looking dreadfully cute and sweet, she almost fled.

"Ah, there she is," the man who must've been Wolfe said, his accent far more prominent than Lyons's, as if he relished it.

They exchanged greetings and pleasantries, taking a seat at the table where he'd brought tall coffees along with various packets of sweetener and cream.

Yep, this was definitely weird. "I feel like you're buttering me up for something. It's okay if you're coming to tell me to lay off the gifts. I think maybe I should after the way yesterday went, even if I have something else I've been making for him."

Wolfe let her ramble, but the dimpled grin in his scruffy jaw and the merriment in his eyes stopped her.

"Not sure what you're talking about." He leaned back in his chair. "I was just hoping to meet the woman Lyons was speaking with. I've been trying to get him to talk about what happened all year, and he usually tells me to shove it in colorful ways."

Angel looked somewhat sheepishly between them. "I actually hadn't told him yet about the gifts."

He nudged Angel lightly. "Fill me in. These are the gifts he's been calling me about?"

Angel's face scrunched up in a way that was cute, and completely chagrined.

"Naughty elf," he murmured, but didn't sound upset with her. "Probably good, it's harder for me to feign ignorance when I'm only sort of ignorant."

"Why are you thinking of stopping now?" Angel asked, slipping her hand into Wolfe's on the table, the casual intimacy so easy between them. It was hard for Belle to even understand for a moment.

"Just he doesn't really speak to me now, except for yesterday when that patient got out of hand."

Wolfe's brows shot up. "And Lyons hit him?"

"No!" Belle blurted out, realized how loud she'd been and lowered her voice. "No, he didn't hit him. He just kind of glowered and threatened him with adult diapers."

"Adult diapers?" Wolfe looked momentarily impressed. "I don't even know how to process that."

"Effectively," Belle said, then rewound to the other question. "And he set the parameters of allowable conversation between us as me being allowed to ask him for advice on medical issues to do with patients but made clear that was it."

"Nothing is ever clear with my brother," Wolfe said, but had started to look somewhat less smiley and charming than he'd been. "I've been hoping to get him to come up-state with us for Christmas, but he's not even interested in coming to dinner before then. I don't—"

His words abruptly died as a door opened behind her, and it took a good long second to summon a smile again. "Hey, coffee?"

Lyons. She didn't even need to look over her shoulder to know it was Lyons. Wolfe had the look of someone busted doing something he shouldn't, and his untouched coffee offer was an olive branch.

Lyons was so quiet that her nerve faltered, and she turned in her chair to look back at him, just to see how bad this was about to become.

He said nothing for long enough that they all got he was containing himself, she just didn't know why.

It was weird that Wolfe was continually reaching out to Lyons and Lyons didn't reach back. Turning down offers to dinner. Not talking about the thing with his friend's murder when he clearly needed to talk about it.

When the glowering man spun and wordlessly marched back out, it stopped being odd to her and turned into some-thing cruel. She was hurt on Wolfe's behalf. And *her* be-half. How could he turn his nose up at family who clearly loved him when other people would do anything for more time with their families? His friend had died, he worked in an emergency room, he *knew* how short life could be.

"Pardon me, ladies," Wolfe muttered, standing to follow Lyons out of the room.

When she looked at Angel then, she could see her own thoughts mirrored there, or at least the emotion behind them. Angel looked like someone who didn't know whether to shout or cry.

* * *

Lyons reached the corridor outside the break room, a number of thoughts bouncing off the inside of his head, but the most prominent one being that this was a set-up. Whatever feelings Belle had about him, his brother had a hand in.

It would certainly make his life easier, if he knew whatever Belle was up to was just kindness she and Angel had cooked up. Maybe they were old friends. Maybe this wasn't just a roll of the dice, her ending up at Sutcliffe.

His face felt hot. He should take a beat and get himself under control before he punched his brother, even if it bothered him how easily his thoughts had begun turning to violence lately.

Yesterday he'd damned near pummeled the hockey player. Today he wanted to punch his brother's perpetually smirking face.

He was losing it.

The door opened, and Lyons turned back, and found Wolfe—cup of coffee in hand—gently closing the door to the break room. However little Wolfe liked to claim he knew him, he knew an added sound barrier would be good.

"By the color of your face, I can tell you need this," Wolfe said, holding out the cup of coffee. "Drink. I don't know what you're thinking, but whatever you think is going on, isn't."

Lyons took the coffee, still quite warm in his hand, and got a drink of a better brew than he'd been about to pour himself. "She's the one giving the gifts, isn't she? She and Angel have worked this little scheme out between them. What's the outcome? Land a wealthy boyfriend?"

"Stop." Wolfe was so calm, Lyons wanted to hit him again.

Instead, he took a bigger, mouth-burning drink of the coffee. "That's not a denial."

"Do you want to do this here?"

Lyons looked at the door, and then at his little brother.

Yes, he wanted to do this here. The women were the only ones in the break room, and this corridor was long enough that if they controlled the volume, it wouldn't be known the hospital over.

"Just answer the damn question."

"They're not scheming," Wolfe grunted. "They *are* friends. And yes, Belle's the one leaving you gifts. I just found out when she asked if she should stop."

"Of course, she should stop. Why the hell is she doing it?"

"Because you're such an ass she thinks you need someone to be kind to you without any expectations of having it returned." Wolfe gestured behind him to the door but kept his voice low, and said more gently, as if he were *fragile*, "She's not our mother. She's not a user."

"She might just be waiting to come out with *whatever* when she thinks I've been softened up."

How stupid could Wolfe be? Gullible. Granted, Wolfe had never known the depths of how far their mother would go to get what she wanted—Lyons had made sure of that beginning when he was old enough to understand himself, but he'd always known enough to *suspect*. He still knew. Everyone hid some kind of selfish darkness. Their mother had just become more honest about it the more desperate she became to stay with their equally dismal human being of a father during their many public, shameful affairs and near divorces.

Wolfe leaned against the wall. "You're wrong. I know you've got your reasons to think as ya do, but you're wrong about Angel, and you're wrong about Belle."

"She made tablet," Lyons muttered, jerking his head in the general direction of the locker room, which wasn't anywhere near where they stood. "She made tablet, she left a gift card, she dropped off a humorous book about Christmas sucking."

"She made tablet!"

That would be the part that got Wolfe's attention. They'd neither one been home in years but would've eaten their weight in the sugary treat as children if they'd been allowed.

"Aye."

"Is it good?"

"Haven't eaten it."

"What?" Wolfe flung his head back dramatically. "Tell me you didn't throw it out."

"It's in my locker." Lyons should've thrown it out. Or given it back to her with orders to stop. Instead, here he stood, arguing with his brother.

Wolfe's hand shot out. "Key."

"What?" It was his turn to look as if his brother were a madman.

"If you're not eating it, I will. She went to the trouble."

They seemed to be on friendly terms, and Belle and Angel were definitely on friendly terms, but not understanding why she'd do this made it even harder to accept.

Still, giving it to Wolfe would get it out of his locker.

He started off down the hallway, and heard Wolfe fall into step with him.

They didn't speak again until Lyons opened the door to his locker and Wolfe pulled the lid off the decorative box that had been waiting for him this morning.

The groan of pleasure he gave before he even took a bite made Lyons want to punch him again.

Wolfe took two pieces, one to throw wholesale into his mouth, and another to follow it after he'd moaned his way through eating the first. "Eat it. It's good. God bless her."

Lyons didn't. "How did she know? I've never met an American who makes the stuff, and she just randomly makes it?"

"She probably went online and looked for sweets from Scotland."

"Or maybe your girlfriend is more involved than you think."

Wolfe eyed him, but didn't stop eating. "If Angel were involved, and she's not, she'd be helping because she wants you to be a little happier. If you want to know Belle's reasons, ask her."

He snagged two more small squares then closed the lid and the locker door, leaving Lyons with the lot of it. And his mouth watering.

"If you start feeling wrong, come down to Emergency."

"She hasn't poisoned it, you daft, paranoid fool." Wolfe shook his head, then just turned to leave with the handful of sugary squares. Before he rounded the bank of lockers, Wolfe looked back and grinned. "Dinner invitation stands. If you want to come wonder if someone else is going to poison ya. I did have that coffee in my hand for about five minutes before you showed up. I could've put anything in there. Rufied you so Belle could have her wicked way."

"Shut it."

"You need it."

Lyons rolled his eyes but didn't follow his brother back out or take the bait. He had coffee to drink, and already felt foolish enough after having heard one of his many entirely irrational suspicions put into words.

Maybe he just should put all his irrational suspicions into words, if hearing them out loud would quell them. It certainly helped see the absolute ridiculousness of *this* situation.

Opening the locker again, he snagged a piece of the candy and took a bite before he had time to think about it.

It was so good he immediately wished he'd not eaten it.

She had to at least be softening him up to *something*. Maybe he should just let her keep softening him up. Take the pleasure and sweetness she offered with an eye on the horizon, and whatever underhanded thing he knew was coming.

His little brother might be annoying, but he wasn't wrong about one thing: he needed at least one night with her. And damn the consequences.

CHAPTER NINE

LYONS HAD AVOIDED Belle since the hockey player post-game yesterday, needing the time to think over what he wanted to do about her. Even though he suspected he would, and did, have another gift waiting for him this morning. She was still giving him gifts even though they weren't really speaking at present. Incomprehensible.

Lyons didn't like to bring scandal into the department. Or the hospital, frankly, but work was his point of contact for Belle.

Wolfe thought he was being foolish, but Wolfe was blinded by love right now and all roads led to a happy place. Lyons just didn't know what to think anymore, didn't trust his gut right now. He could recognize that the closer he came to Christmas, the more his thinking tilted toward the negative, but that didn't mean he was wrong.

What he did know was wrong was to allow this to continue after the gift that had been waiting for him this morning. Something she'd obviously put a great deal of work into.

He wasn't much bothered by clothing; he was a very standard kind of bloke. He went for traditional styles in everything. Hired someone to make sure he had what he needed. He took no interest, past being able to discern quality when he saw it.

This morning's gift had been handmade from quality materials. It was tucked into a little Christmas gift bag, giving no indication that she'd purchased it somewhere, and considering she'd made yesterday's tablet, he knew she'd made it as well.

The only civilized thing to do was to give her a chance to explain and tell her politely to stop. Or if she denied it, tell her he'd report her to HR if she didn't stop.

He made it to the cafeteria and it took no time to find her once again at that small table, her back to the room. The woman was never going to learn, and if she was so lax about security at home...

No. Focus.

He cut his way across the cafeteria, pulled out a chair and sat, catching her mid-bite.

She made some noise of alarm, and then chewed fast, dark eyes wide and focused on him as if expecting an attack.

He let her finish before saying anything.

"Lyons." She coughed lightly, then reached for her water.

"You don't have to swallow so fast you choke yourself," he said, and then gestured to the room. "And if you'd sat with your back to the wall there, you'd have seen me coming."

Last time he'd bring that up.

"I like the secluded feeling of facing the wall over facing the whole cafeteria."

"It's some kind of social distancing?"

She shrugged. "I brought my headphones to block out the noise too but thought it would get in the way of eating."

"Don't do that," he muttered, and then shook his head and scooted his chair sideways so he could better see the rest of the large room. He waited for her to finish another drink of her water, but she didn't go back to her lunch. He'd successfully claimed her attention, and the civilized thing to do would be to get this done quickly so she could finish eating before she went back to work.

Probably because he'd been avoiding her, she prompted, "Something on your mind?"

"Are you leaving me gifts at my locker every morning?"

To her credit, her cheeks pinked a bit and she looked away for a second but looked him in the eye again before nodding. "Are you angry?"

"No." The word came reflexively, and momentarily surprised him. "Why are you doing it?"

"You won't like the answer." Her voice had taken on a slightly sing-song quality, but the song it sang was chagrin.

"Tell me anyway."

"My grandmother, Dad's mom, was like our second parent. My mom walked out when we were really little. Then after Dad...we went to live with Nanna full-time. And she did it when we were little, but I remember her saying it even more after Dad was shot."

Her warning had sounded as if he wouldn't like the reason because it was about him, but even before it became about him, he didn't like it. Her father was dead, her mother had left them, and her grandmother...was she alive? No, he didn't think so. She'd referred to her grandmother in the past tense: she *was* like our second parent.

It was just her and her sister?

Her eyes were sad, and she looked away from him—not with purpose, it was more as if she fell into memories held in the middle distance between what was right in front of her, and the cafeteria table she looked through.

Whatever she was about to say felt heavier because he knew it was related to family she'd lost, but he still wasn't prepared for when she touched his arm and turned those deep, soulful eyes to his.

"People who hurt others, who lash out, are suffering and need the most kindness."

There was no accusation in her voice, and, although he should probably have been offended, somehow it felt like an intervention. Like someone who cared so much for him she'd just opened herself up to attack and ridicule.

What could he say in response to the sincerity that rang in her voice and her touch?

"It's dangerous to feel that way, Belle. Why would you think that?"

"Because it's true. I've seen it happen."

"No…"

"I've also seen it fail," she said quickly, clearly anticipating the argument. "My nanna said it to us after Mom left, and all the time when we went to live with her after Dad died. She didn't want us to become bitter or lose faith in people."

"How is putting you in danger helping you?"

"Because it was too late for my mom," she said, then squeezed his arm. "But it's not too late for you."

The soft words—even expressing a sentiment he'd heard between the lines—knocked the air out of him, her eyes so full of compassion, and something else, something that made his throat ache with something he couldn't swallow past.

She saw and removed her hand to pass him her water in offering. He took it wordlessly and drank until he could speak again.

"What makes you think that?" He didn't think that; the only reason she would was because she didn't know him.

"How is the patient who was injured in the subway derailment?"

She knew he'd kept up. And the tiny, rueful smile she wore said she knew he *still* kept up.

"That doesn't mean anything." Except that he was good at his job and took his responsibility seriously.

"It means you care. Even when he ceased to be your patient or responsibility," she countered. "And I saw tears in your eyes when you couldn't get Mrs. Martinez's heart going. That wasn't just about your friend."

When he'd imagined this conversation, it had been much

more defensive and angry, not something that left *him* feeling the ground unsteady beneath his feet.

All that he'd said, he still hadn't thanked her.

She might still have some darkness she was hiding, but maybe he could get through Christmas with her, and help her get through it without having family here with her.

"Do you want to have dinner?" he asked suddenly, the words just coming out of his mouth as they formed in his head.

Her eyes sprang wide open then and it took her a couple of seconds to blink her way through the surprise she completely failed to conceal. "Outside of work?"

"That's when I usually eat dinner." He turned his arm and slid it back, so her hand glided down to his palm where he could wrap his fingers around her small, delicate hand.

She didn't immediately answer but shifted her gaze to their joined hands and thought for several seconds.

"I'll have dinner with you on two conditions."

Conditions for dinner. Here it came. He tried to keep his posture easy, though he felt that stiffness creeping into his shoulders again. He'd almost fallen for it…of course she wanted something in return for gracing him with her company.

"That you come to my apartment and I cook dinner," she said. "I haven't been able to bring myself to make some of my favorite foods because the way I know how to make things ends up with far too much food and I don't want to be wasteful. If you come over and eat it, it's not wasted."

"You want to cook for me again?"

That wasn't what he'd expected. At all. Were all his instincts wrong?

"I want to cook, period."

He nodded, containing his relief until she'd given her other condition. "Second?"

"Be nicer to your brother." She said the words incredibly

softly, as if she was almost afraid it would bring out some kind of explosion.

"I'm not mean to Wolfe."

"You're not *kind* to him either."

Still, not a condition that was for *her*. God, he wanted to believe she was just that selfless.

And shone a light on how selfish it was for him to keep Wolfe at bay. "I'll try. It's been hard this year."

"I understand the desire to wall yourself off from others when you've been through something really painful, but I think he needs you."

"It's not that," he admitted. "I just haven't felt anything but angry for a long time."

She turned her hand and shifted her chair closer so that she could lace her fingers between his. "But you feel that."

The touch. Yes, he felt that.

"I'll try harder with Wolfe."

It wasn't a promise, but it was as much as he could offer.

"How do you feel about manicotti Friday night?"

Belle had spent two days mentally preparing for the dinner. Making lists when she had a moment to spare, working out the order she'd need to make the dishes to get them done in the shortest time.

Out of work at three, she walked into her apartment at almost five, carrying two bags of groceries, and didn't stop moving until the main entrance to the building buzzed at eight, announcing Lyons's arrival. Because she'd gone overboard.

It was as if her desire to make the dinner had made her forget what time meant: cooking that massive a Natal dinner took two days. It just did. She had to whittle like crazy to get the menu down to something manageable that would still tick the boxes.

She was just glad she'd managed to sneak in a lightning-fast shower to rid herself of that just-dipped-in-antiseptic hospital smell, and allowed a whirlwind through the still-packed box of underthings to find the sexiest scrap of lace she owned. Stuff she'd never worn. Stuff she'd managed to purchase in honor of Noelle last Christmas, which was probably really psychologically wrong, but which had remained packed up until this evening.

Just-in-case underwear.

The man kissed like a five-alarm fire, and even when she'd been upset with him, that kiss, and all the rest of it, had kept creeping into her thoughts. If things got sexy after dinner, she could only pray she could steal five minutes to tidy up before he saw the mess.

Hold that thought, big boy. I have to tidy my room before we can do The Thing.

Or what was probably more likely: he'd eat in a very cool and efficient manner, dodge all questions except those pertaining to work and then go home. But a girl had to have hope.

Because no matter what she felt about establishing long-term relationships with anyone, she needed *closeness*. The whole point of keeping from diving in with her whole heart was to avoid suffering, not to switch one suffering out for another form.

It was the second ring at her apartment door; she shuffled down the hallway, tugging on her top and tossing the last curler from her bangs into the hall closet—the last mad scramble of a Nervous Nelly to become presentable.

"Sorry!" she blurted out as she swung the door open.

She was used to seeing him in scrubs, and, although she had seen him half changed before, seeing him in well-fitting jeans, black leather coat, and the gray hat and scarf set she'd knitted him just about knocked her flat.

"I was going to give you one more ring before calling the police." He had a bottle of wine in hand and a grumpy look on his face, but he did step through the door she held open wide.

"Well, thank you for the lengths you considered going to for my safety, but I probably couldn't have gotten into too much trouble between buzzing you in and opening the door." She helped him out of his coat and the woolies she'd made, and hung them in the closet.

"You must have done something—you're pink-cheeked and breathless." He handed her the wine, and, before she could answer, turned his back to her so he could engage every lock on the door and then give the thing a vigorous rattle. "I don't like your door. It's not very sturdy."

"Lyons?" When he looked back in response to hearing his name, she caught him by the cheek and stood on tiptoe to press her lips to his. Distraction, delightful distraction, and a reminder what he was there for: spend time with her, not inspect her door.

And it worked. He turned more fully toward her, hands settling on her hips to tug her to him, then wound his arms around her.

Unlike their first kiss, which had exploded like a match in an oxygen tent, this time when he took control and kissed her back, it was slowly. His arms held her tight to him, solid, warm and strong enough to cause silly romantic images to spin to life in her mind about what it'd be like to be carried by him. Her arms around his neck, she could feel his restraint; he held tight and kissed slowly, as if he had all the time in the world and this wasn't a simple kiss for greeting.

The other kiss was driven by lust and need. This one, she felt more. Not just need to block out something painful. Kissed because he wanted *her*, not just relief to his pain.

She'd kissed him because she'd really wanted to, not only because he'd worn the woolies she'd made him and that showed appreciation, they meant something to him, but also because she'd wanted to distract him from the door.

She clutched tighter at his shoulders, wanting closer still, so aware in that second of how terribly lonely the past year had been. Like the difference in reading about the ocean and wading in the surf. His touch, his presence, the sound of his breathing, the heat of his skin—the *life* pulsing through him was a spotlight, making clear how much of her life she'd been spending in darkness.

And she didn't know the fix for that without making herself one bad day away from losing everything again. It happened, and, no matter how superstitious she knew it sounded, if he wasn't hers, she couldn't lose him.

There was no arguing with heartbreak. Logic and reason caved to the internal echo of "What if?" What if it happened to every person she ever had the audacity to love?

Her lower lip quivered against his kiss and he drew back immediately. She pulled her arms free and dropped her eyes so he wouldn't see it.

"Hey…"

Not seeing didn't help. She could hear the concern in his voice.

She gestured toward the kitchen. "I need to check dinner."

"Wait." He snagged her hand and kept her in place. "Are you crying?"

"No," she said. A lie, because if she explained what had just happened it would completely ruin the whole evening. She danced around the subject of Noelle because she couldn't bring herself to say the words. Pretended Noelle was just away—that was how she got through her days.

God, she was a terrible date.

She wiggled her hand free. "I'm sorry. The manicotti will be done soon. I just need a minute. Unless you want to hang out with a woman who is suddenly crying."

"Crying when I kissed her," he corrected, but there was no censure in his voice. He just gave a tug and wrapped his arms around her again, leaving her arms folded against his chest and her face tucked under that immaculate jaw.

"It's not that. And I started the kissing," she whispered. "I just got a little overwhelmed suddenly."

Another lie. Not a terrible one—she did get over-whelmed—she just couldn't explain why.

"You don't want to tell me?" he asked, but his arms didn't waver. He didn't thrust her away, even when she shook her head.

"But you want me to talk to you."

Not a question but loaded all the same.

"Yes, but you don't have to."

"I know Wolfe asked you to get me to talk."

"He didn't." She leaned back then, just enough to look him in the eye.

His eyebrows called her a liar.

"He didn't *exactly* say that," she corrected. "He just said he hoped that you were able to talk to someone, but he'd rather it was him, you know."

He made some sound of affirmation, rubbed her back a little, then let go. "Where's the fire escape?"

Subject change. Whatever, she'd take it.

She gestured toward the living room, and he let go of her to go prowling in that direction.

"Why do you need the fire escape?" she asked, then she remembered the manicotti, which she'd die if she burned.

She rushed into the kitchen in time to see the last seven seconds on her timer, shut it off, pulled the dish from the oven and rejoined Lyons at the fire escape.

The busyness helped settle her thoughts and tear ducts too. His sudden fixation on her fire escape also helped.

She found him rattling the window and checking the lock. "Also not as sturdy as I'd like."

"They're plenty sturdy." She covered his window-rattling hand with hers and tried to slide between him and the window.

"It's not the best neighborhood."

"It's a perfectly fine neighborhood. Is your neighbor-hood so much better? I mean, I know you're a doctor and that means you do well, but, really, this is a solidly higher-end middle-class neighborhood. It's just an older building."

He turned toward her, his brows halfway up his forehead. For the first time since she'd known him, he looked completely shocked. He always looked as if the world both conformed to his expectations and entirely disappointed him. "You don't know where I live?"

"I leave presents at your locker. I'm not a stalker who followed you home to leave them at your front door."

This silly, teasing way of answering didn't remove the look or the incredulity in his voice.

"Yes, but, no one told you? Conley?"

"Angel," she corrected. "Her name is Angel."

"Fine. Didn't Angel tell you?"

"Why would Angel, or anyone, tell me where you live?" That said, this whole thing was starting to feel ominous. "Why? Where do you live?"

"I live on Park. In a large, modern building."

"Park Avenue?" she asked, unable to keep her own incredulity out. Even she knew what *Park* meant.

"Our family has some businesses."

"What kind of businesses?"

"Show me the other windows," he said instead. "Because I'm clearly going to have to barter information with you. You show me the rest of the apartment, answer my questions, and I will answer your questions."

The tears. That was the question he wanted. But if he had information to barter, she *didn't* know the whole story about his lousy Christmas.

"All my questions?"

He hesitated for only a second, then nodded.

Dammit.

"The only other windows are in the bedroom."

Where it looked as if a lingerie shop had exploded. And a yarn shop. And possibly a hair salon—she wasn't sure where all those curlers had landed in her mad rush to finish dressing between the entry-door buzzer and her doorbell.

"Lead the way."

With a flap of her arms, she headed to the other room in her small apartment. "It's kind of messy."

"Messy?"

"Well, I had a gift card."

Which she'd bought for her sister because Noelle loved lingerie, but had then felt compelled to use because she clearly had no idea how to handle grief like an adult.

His footfalls behind her stopped, at the door, prompting her to look over her shoulder at him. He was smiling. Not just a small grin, as they'd shared when joking about furious bunnies, but a big, toothy smile. "Did you have a lingerie shopping spree?"

"Last year. It was all boxed up. And I'm not done moving."

"But you felt compelled to unpack that box tonight."

If he was handsome under the worst conditions, smiling that broadly with his eyes full of mischief, he was devastating. She felt it like lightning down her spine, melting in her belly.

"Maybe." She grabbed a bra and the matching panties she'd tried on and dropped on the floor, then another. And the baby-doll nightie, she stuffed that right up her shirt. Out of sight! Obviously, she was insane and her stealth and subtlety education lacking—he watched her doing it.

Because he was right behind her. Laughing.

"I'm getting laid. That's what you brought me to your lair for, you she-wolf."

"Shut up!" She grabbed a bra she *hadn't* tried on and flung it at his face.

He caught it easily, and his laughter only slowed as he examined the lacy red cups on the way to the first window, and casually handed it to her as he passed by.

She left him with the windows to stash the lingerie in drawers.

Like the living room, he opened the drapes, opened and closed the locks, opened and closed the windows too—for reasons she couldn't even pretend to understand—and then locked back up again.

"What businesses are your people in?" she asked, moving over to nudge him toward the door.

"Many different businesses over the decades, but most recently aviation and aerospace."

His answer could have flattened her if she hadn't been held up and animated by complete mortification of the bra room. The boredom she heard in his voice somehow made it more fantastical, as if aerospace were the most mundane, trivial thing ever. He and Wolfe were doctors, but their family apparently built…spaceships! Or probably more like satellites. And planes. Winged things.

Park Avenue son, and maybe *heir* to some aerospace company. She was really glad she'd got the panettone, even if she'd had no time to make the bread pudding she'd planned. This was *not* what she'd been picturing when she'd agreed to a date. Not that they had a future together, but, still, it was nice to know what you were getting before you decided whether to get it or not. She'd just thought he was a sexy, talented doctor with terrible people skills.

"I'm pretty sure you're going to be disappointed by dinner." She stopped attempting to plow him out of the room and glanced down the hallway to where she'd placed the wine before this tour of windows had started. "Because it's good, but a five-star chef I am not."

He took the hint and guided her back down the hall, plucking the wine from the table as they moved past it to the kitchen.

What else was she supposed to be doing? Felt like a weird

gear shift to go directly from some inexplicable home inspection to eating.

"Hey?" His voice came from the other room.

She grabbed the corkscrew and came back from the kitchen to find him staring at a portrait Noelle had drawn of the two of them, replicated from a tropical Christmas selfie from a couple of years ago, in colored pencil on a golden-brown paper so the light leads would pop. The last one Noelle had given her.

"You're a twin."

"Yeah. Noelle, Ysabelle. I thought that was pretty obvious." She knew she looked like the make-up-free version of her sister. They could be…could've been… *Before* and *After* makeover photos.

"You never told me her name is Noelle."

Was.

She couldn't get her thinking right tonight, screwing up verb tenses.

"I didn't?" She actually hadn't realized that. "Well, yeah. Twins. She was the pretty one." There were several of Noelle's portraits lining the living room, all drawn from photos when she was away, and running in age from apple-cheeked toddlers to the one he'd started with.

He'd moved to another portrait, the unopened wine still in his hand. She hadn't unpacked all her things, but she had gotten her portraits and photos on the walls and had done before she'd even unpacked her kitchen. The rest of the apartment was relatively spartan—she moved with the smallest effort possible—but her walls were alive with memories.

"I can't tell which one is you."

Was.

She didn't correct him aloud, the word just shot through her, impossible to ignore.

"Left." She'd always stood on the same side. "Dinner is done. Can you open the wine?"

He had moved on to a picture of them with their grandmother from more than a decade ago. "How old are you?"

"Thirty-three."

He shook his head. "In this picture?"

She tilted her head at the photo. It had been a few months before Nanna had passed. "Twenty-one."

He took the corkscrew she held out to him and having something to do did get him moving. She gestured for him to follow, and didn't stop moving until they were seated, the table was loaded and the wine poured.

"I'm trying to imagine why Noelle isn't here this Christmas," Lyons said, his voice sober. "And I think it's part of why you get so upset about Wolfe and me not being close. You two are fighting about something?"

He spoke, and then finally took a bite of the manicotti, skipping right over the other courses in favor of the star attraction. The look on his face made it easier to pretend he hadn't just said something completely insane. And to avoid answering. She didn't want to talk about her sister.

"Good?"

"Five-star." He took another bite and watched her the whole time.

As if that was going to make her crumble. She'd seen him cold and shouting. Eyeing her while he enjoyed her family recipes? Nothing intimidating in that.

On second thought, that was not the look in his eyes. He might genuinely be enjoying the food, but was already thinking ahead to her lingerie bomb and dessert.

Dessert was easy to think of when he watched her through those half-lowered lids, eyes gleaming with intent.

Belle's breath sped up just from the way he watched her. Every other time he'd felt attracted, she'd known it by the intent looks being followed by a glare. She knew how to deal with that reaction. But this made her overly hurried and graceless; every bite came with the strong possibility she'd accidentally choke to death if he didn't stop.

"Did you talk to Wolfe?" Smooth subject change, score even.

"I told him I'd come for dinner when they got back from their holiday," he answered.

That brought her smile back.

"Where's Noelle?"

And there went her smile, along with her appetite.

"Still not going to talk, eh?"

"I just want to enjoy dinner with you."

"Then eat, because this food is too good to waste, and I have questions."

CHAPTER TEN

UNTIL SHE'D ASKED about Wolfe, Lyons had been planning a different route through the evening—one that ended, in his head, with him convincing her to model the lingerie strewn all over her room.

Then, despite dinner being delicious, and the possibility of all the other delicacies she had to sample, he forced his focus on the conversation they needed to have. "Are you done?"

"Tasted better in my memory."

"And here I thought you were dreading my asking questions, and prolonging dinner."

"That too."

Scooting the chair back, he gestured, beckoning her with one hand. "I can make it easier."

"No one can make it easier," she whispered, but didn't hesitate coming to stand beside him, and placed her hand in the hand he offered.

Despite the turmoil in her eyes, just like every time they touched, peace flowed from her. But she needed to *accept* comfort tonight, not give it. He could pretend in that she was as good as she seemed. For tonight.

Even if she didn't return the sentiment about needing to talk about whatever was hurting her, he was going to talk first. Ease her into it.

And he'd have her in his arms meanwhile.

It only took a little prompting for her to slide into his lap. She sat crossways, one arm around his shoulders and the other hand draped across her lap, holding the hand she'd originally taken.

"I know you don't talk about whatever happened, so I'll go first."

One look into her eyes said she was thinking about whatever had happened that made her bribe her sister with photos of New York—what else could set up that situation?

He knew too well how easily thoughts returned to a painful subject if not controlled. It took far more effort to stay out of the memories, and he saw that effort mirrored in her face. And then he saw her lift her chin and give him a half nod to continue.

Lyons didn't know when he'd decided to talk to her—it was some time since she'd basically told him that she believed in him—and he didn't know if he just wanted to tell her for the benefit of his own soul, or the benefit of hers so she could get away and stop trying to make him better.

In those seconds while she held his gaze, he couldn't think of where to begin. What he did know was that she felt good on his lap, and she smelled of cinnamon and peaches—a strange mix he couldn't quite believe worked so well on her skin.

"Do you want me to ask questions?"

"No. Thinking of where to start."

"With your friend?"

"Eleni," he answered and went with it, all the while watching her eyes for the censure that had to be coming. "She was an emergency specialist too. Was leaving her husband. He abused her. I'd offered to help her get away. Christmas Eve he got angry, and she finally made her decision, showed up in Emergency. I always worked Christmas, so that's where she came."

"You were dating?"

"No," he said too strongly, judging by the way she recoiled slightly. He tried again, more quietly. "She was married. My parents are infamous for their affairs and scandals. I have a very low view of people who cheat and the damage it does."

His heart rate had already started to pick up and he hadn't even gotten to the part of the memory that kept him from ever discussing what happened. Because when he said the words, when he even thought them, there was no way to avoid seeing it, and his body reacted the same as it had at the time.

"And he shot her in the ER?"

She just blurted it out, and suddenly the air in the room thickened like a dense fog, and his body reacted by breathing hard and far too shallow.

"I tried to get the gun. Told her to run. But I didn't get it." He spoke in bursts, breathing too frequently. "He shot her in the back. As she ran away."

"You're breathing too fast." Her eyes had widened, and now flickered over his face as the arm around his neck curled so she could reach her fingers to a pulse point on the side. "You have to slow it down. Head between your legs."

He grabbed her before she could get up. "No. If I stop now, I won't finish."

She frowned, but nodded and gestured for him to hurry. "He shot me first."

Both of her arms retracted so she could cover her face with both hands, trying to muffle the sob that wrenched out of her.

Just the one, and she removed her hands to grab his shoulders. "Where? Leg? Arm?"

She forgot his breathing, and he did too. Her undisguised distress, not disgust or castigation, sank in better than being coddled and held had done.

He caught one hand and placed it over his left upper chest, a place hidden by his clothes.

Past that big, gut-punching sob, she quieted but tears

continued to stream from her eyes. She leaned back, hands going to the waist of his jumper and jerking up. "Can I see? Can you just show me?"

She found the three scarred holes puckering his chest and shoulder, then stroked and petted over them with cool fingertips while her other arm slid around him to search his back for exit wounds.

He let her; she was openly crying now and he didn't have it in him to say anything else.

Had his brother cried when it had happened? Would *he* be able to mourn for Wolfe if he suffered now?

Yes. The idea of Wolfe being shot made an ache sink in his chest he wasn't sure he'd have been capable of feeling even a week ago. The same place that wanted her distress to end, but which he knew he couldn't let go of now. He needed to know what ate at her.

"One…"

Her fingers sought blindly on his back.

"Two…

"Three."

They all exited.

She twisted on his lap to flatten her chest to his, her arms around his shoulders to squeeze as tight as her trembling arms would allow.

"What happened with Noelle?" He said the words as gently as he could, one hand cupping the back of her head and burrowing into her silky hair.

She shook harder and he held tighter, listening to her breaths coming in tremulous gasps.

God, she was fighting it. And the harder she did, the larger the hole in his chest grew.

The wetness rushing over his bare shoulder was going to kill him, and that drove home how much more he was feeling for her. He couldn't ask again.

Didn't have to. He knew: Noelle had died.

"I'm sorry." He offered the only words he had to give,

that and holding and rocking. Her touch comforted him—he doubted his would be as beneficial, but he had to do something.

She rocked with him, fluid, and the longer it went, the more she relaxed against him. Her hiccups subsided, settling into sniffing.

Without prompting, she said, "It was a fluke, like a lightning strike. MRSA urinary tract infection."

His heart sank. Bladder infections seemed like the last thing that could make someone go septic, but it happened to young, otherwise healthy people with disturbing frequency. But it *felt* like a lightning strike. "Didn't respond to treatment?"

"It was silent until it had already spread beyond her bladder. She felt more like she'd just had a random virus." She tilted her head so her cheek rested on his shoulder. "She was a pilot, and all that time in airports and on planes with recirculating air, she got sick a lot."

He squeezed, not knowing what else to say to her. Wanting to stop…but the emails. The pictures. He couldn't leave it at that. "When did it happen?"

"Last year." Whispers. Her voice had fallen to whispers.

"Christmas?"

"No." She swallowed. "July."

"The pictures?" he asked, just to get it done.

"Her email still works." The trembling in her body started again. "I know I should stop. I thought maybe after Christmas."

That was her coping mechanism. He couldn't fix this. The best he could do was make sure she didn't spend Christmas alone.

"Will you stay tonight?" she asked, voice soft, barely more than a breath, and pulled back to look at him, eyes red and damp. "But, I don't feel very sexy right now."

She didn't want to be alone with it. He didn't either.

"I'll stay."

She pressed forward and kissed him, her lips soft, seeking and giving comfort. Sweet. Loving. He felt it burning in his chest, where her hand still rested over two of the scars, as if she could protect those old wounds by covering them.

"I think I need you to hide my phone," she said against his lips.

"Hmm?"

"Turn it off, put it somewhere I can't find it for tonight. I still want to email her because it makes me feel better."

"Do you want to stop or are you feeling the need to keep up appearances by stopping?"

"I know it's unhealthy. But if I'm not alone, I think I can stop."

She didn't say she felt better because it was *him*, just by having someone. That pinched a bit, until he remembered how bad he tended to be with relationships after the abysmal examples he had with his parents, and accepted her just needing someone was better than needing *him*.

"Get the phone," he said, reluctantly relaxing his arms so she could retrieve it.

She made sure it was turned off, then handed it to him. "I'll put dinner up, and I just kind of want to go to sleep. Is that okay?"

He looked at the pretty rose-gold phone in his hand, and nodded, then cleared his throat and asked one more question. "Is that why you always have your nose in your phone in the cafeteria and locker room?"

"Sometimes," she answered. "Sometimes I'm reading the books you told me to read."

Then she went to the kitchen and busied herself with containers and rolls of foil, or plastic, or something. He stood, leaving his tops where they'd fallen on the floor, and went in search of a hiding place.

Lyons awoke the next morning with Belle sprawled, face down, over his chest, her feet hanging off the edge of the bed and her cheek propped on his shoulder, facing away. The hair he'd known would be miles of silk half covered his face. But he still felt himself smile as he gathered the tresses and tucked it under his chin.

She was not a sleeping angel. There was nothing peaceful or quiet about her slumber. It didn't seem to be restlessness spawned by bad dreams; she just moved a lot. And at one point, she might have been talking to a pet. At least he hoped she was talking to a pet, because that was definitely baby talk.

He'd awakened once to find her hand covering the scars on his still-bare chest, the thickest knot of flesh directly in the hollow of her palm. It felt deliberate, even in sleep. It gave him a feeling he could neither name nor decide what to do with.

They'd sleep easier in the same bed tonight. Or maybe they wouldn't. He hadn't really considered anything beyond last night.

She stirred and lifted off him to look down, her eyes sleepy, and still a little pink from last night's difficult conversation.

"I'm lying on top of you," she mumbled in a sleepy voice. "Did I talk?"

"Mmm-hmm."

"Did I sing?"

"You sing while asleep?" Even as the words came, he could picture it, and smiled again.

"Not very often. Noelle said I meowed at her once."

He laughed out loud then.

"I'm hungry. I bought panettone yesterday and ran out of time to make bread pudding."

Two thoughts that did not seem to go together. "You're making bread pudding now?"

"French toast." She rubbed her eyes, stretched once loud and long, then sprang from the bed in the cute little shorts and tee shirt she wore to jiggle off, presumably to the kitchen.

He hadn't gotten to see any underwear show, or even suggest it. Things had not gone down that road, and her little jiggling rear made him curse himself and lie in bed a few more minutes until his body settled down.

When he got to the kitchen, she'd already pulled her hair back in a knotted ponytail and had a pan heating on the stove while she sliced the bread. Eggs, milk, sugar and cinnamon sat in a clump on the counter, ready to be assembled. He washed up and went to help.

"How many eggs?"

"Three," she answered, grinning as she rattled off the other ingredients and measurements he'd never be able to get right—*about* this much of this…*about* that much of that.

When he grumbled about it, she asked, "Didn't you ever cook before?"

"Infrequently."

"Because you have people who cook, right?"

"Because I have a lady who stocks my fridge with meals that just need warming up."

"Spoiled."

"Mmm-hmm."

"Why did you come here from Scotland? And when? Your accent only appears here and there, but Wolfe's is very prominent." She'd awakened quite chatty, and in a much better mood than she'd gone to sleep in, which he suddenly remembered he'd been worried about.

"Came for medical school and to get far away from my parents."

"You mentioned their affairs—just tired of the drama?"

"They're not good people."

"Are they like…criminals or something?" She mixed the egg and milk concoction for him.

After he got directions from her on where to find the supplies, he set about making coffee instead.

"Your father was a cop. My parents aren't criminals that I'm aware, they just know no loyalty and have a very unhealthy relationship. They're told no so infrequently they accept no boundaries, even with their children, in getting their way." He tried to explain, but realized she was disturbed but not quite getting it when he looked at her. Knowing she'd lost her family, how deeply she'd loved them, he could see how his family situation sounded alien to her.

"When you have enough money, you get used to having things go the way you want. Doesn't make for good people."

"You didn't turn out that way."

"I get told no often—maybe I missed getting used to having my way. Especially after being raised by them."

He had no real explanation, and thinking about his childhood never gave any peace or happiness, so he avoided it.

"Well, I'm not going to tell you no today. What do you want to do? Do you want to run off home and get away from crazy me, or hang out and eat some more of the massive amounts of food I made yesterday?"

"There's a lot?"

"We could have manicotti for breakfast, lunch and dinner until Monday."

He grinned but went quiet.

He knew what he *wanted* to do, but it seemed wrong to just say: How about we get naked and make up for last night? Because last night hadn't been a failure, it had just gone in a completely different direction than either of them had expected, and left a strange sort of intimacy in its wake.

"Ask me after breakfast. I need time to think something up."

"I'll ask an easier question." She set about dipping the slices of bread and placing them into the pan. If he let her feed him often, he'd gain thirty pounds.

But this was just for the weekend. He swallowed the coffee, which tasted more bitter than the first drink.

"How do the people at Sutcliffe not know that you were shot at your last hospital?"

"Different hospital system, about an hour north of the city," he said, because that had been the agreed-upon answer should anyone ever find out and ask, but it was only part of the story. "To help, Wolfe employed some of our parents' more corrupt practices to keep my name out of the papers."

Her brows shot up, but she didn't say anything out loud, just the questions shooting from her eyes.

"He paid off a lot of people."

"Wolfe?"

Wolfe had done those things because he'd been trying to protect the brother who'd really needed looking after at the time, and Lyons had still distanced himself. He should've accepted the dinner invitation sooner. "All news starts local. It wasn't that hard."

"Wow."

"Don't judge him too harshly. I really didn't want the scrutiny."

"Because you think people would think that the only reason she left her husband was because you were having an affair and blame you?"

"We weren't, but I'm a man, she was a woman. We'd spent a lot of time talking. All it takes is one internet search with my parents' names to see their indiscretions. It would be hard to keep a job if they thought I was having an affair with a colleague and got her killed."

"But you didn't kill her."

The same words Wolfe had said so many times.

"I know."

"If her husband was abusive and shot you both, he was capable of doing it no matter what gave her the strength to try and get free. People like that…" She paused to flip the toast and then looked at him. "Did he go to jail?"

"Killed himself there."

She didn't say anything, but the quiet fury he saw in her face was startling.

"What are you thinking?"

"Torn between being glad he can't hurt anyone else, and wishing you'd been able to confront him for answers." She frowned deeply, then just changed the subject. "Thought about what you want to do with the day?"

Bed.

He almost said the word, but when he opened his mouth, something else came out. "I want to go to Ramapo."

"You want to *what?*"

"I want to go to my old hospital. In Ramapo."

She was quiet for several seconds, busied herself with breakfast, brows tense. "Don't think I'm doubting you can do it, but why do you want to do it now? Why not wait until after Christmas, when it'll be less stressful?"

They discussed the idea until breakfast was fully ready, with Belle firmly in protective mode, and him arguing about hot irons and striking while.

Was he sure?

No.

But before this morning, he'd never had the slightest urge to return. If he waited, he might lose his nerve.

CHAPTER ELEVEN

BELLE DRAGGED HER feet cleaning the kitchen and getting ready after breakfast, which was a really passive-aggressive way of trying to get him to change his mind about going. But about one, he left to get his car and told her to be ready when he came back, or she wasn't coming.

Which was how she found herself on her first road trip out of the city, tense because last night had been so emotionally draining, she selfishly didn't want to dig back into the wound. And she didn't want him to either.

He'd taken it all more stoically, at least until she'd told him about Noelle. Her phone was still hidden somewhere in her apartment, which was some crazy leap of faith to take.

"What's the plan?" she asked, fidgeting with her seat belt, and then with her scarf to keep the belt from rubbing against her neck, and because she needed to fuss. Having something to do with her hands, anything to do with them, would keep her sane. Ish.

"Drive there. Park. Go into Emergency. Say hi if I recognize anyone. Go back to your apartment, spend the rest of the day in bed."

She felt her cheeks heat and, despite her nerves, smiled. "Well, I like most of that plan."

Then, "How much longer?"

"Two exits."

It had taken literally no time. She'd blinked and they'd

gotten there. Where was that New York traffic when she needed it?

He didn't say another word until after he'd driven up every level of the parking garage, past loads of free spaces where they could've parked, and back into the daylight on top.

She didn't want to stare at him, but she couldn't help herself from looking, and when she saw him again in the light of day, his pallor made her neck run cold.

He'd entered the garage a normal shade of pale Scotsman, but six levels later looked as if he'd never seen sunlight before.

Still, he maneuvered the car into a parking spot and turned it off. Said nothing.

"Which building is it?"

He gestured and dropped his hand onto the gear shift. Was he trying to bolster his gumption to complete the trip, or was he looking for a way out?

Give him an out.

She laid her hand over his and squeezed. "You don't have to go in if you don't want to."

"We drove for an hour." It was self-criticism, complaint about him not doing what he'd decided he'd just be able to run right in and do.

"Yes, it was a nice drive." She tried to spin it. "We didn't hear a single Christmas carol on the radio."

"We didn't listen to the radio."

"I didn't spontaneously burst into Christmas carols."

He tried to smile; the corners of his mouth twitched, the tiniest micro-movement, and settled back into that deep, worried frown.

"Let's go." He slid his hand from beneath hers, grabbed the keys from the ignition and climbed out.

She said a little prayer under her breath then scrambled out of the car to go with him. If he was going to go, it wouldn't be alone. She knew about *alone*, and was starting to see she never actually did the hard things alone. Not the emotional work, only the physical. She'd buried her twin on autopilot—picking out a coffin, a dress, flowers, buying a burial plot near Dad and Nanna, ordering a gravestone.

She'd done the things as if they were for a stranger, and left town the day after the funeral. Then *pretended*.

Until last night. With this man. She wouldn't let him face this alone.

That wasn't even counting the people he'd see and what if they said something hideous to him? Although she felt he was on the way to recovery—maybe they both were—he still needed kindness more than anyone she knew. Having hate spewed at him would only make him feel worse.

He waited for her, masking his emotions behind the grim set of his brow, but took her hand and walked resolutely toward the elevators.

When he didn't immediately press the call button, she searched his face again. His jaw—which he'd shaven when he'd gone to fetch his car—gritted so hard it looked as if that muscle at the corner was beating out an SOS.

She could push it for him, but that would be pushing this whole thing another step forward, and he wasn't ready. If he was ready, his subconscious wouldn't be signaling for help through jaw-based Morse code.

"Is there a good place to get coffee in Pomadoo?"

Yeah, she'd said the name wrong, but it was a silly name and that was the pattern, and she couldn't remember the right syllables at that second.

He'd worn the woolen hat she'd knitted again, and she let go of his hand so she could move to stand in front of him and give it a little adjustment, pulling it better over his chill-reddened ears.

"Ramapo," he corrected woodenly, but let her fuss. They hadn't summoned the elevator, but it dinged anyway, announcing the arrival of someone in search of their car.

A disgusted shake of his head followed, and before the

doors opened he took her hand again to walk far too quickly back to the car.

This time, he didn't just let her put herself inside his fancy Infinity. He held the door, and when she sat, he actually fastened the seat belt.

Suddenly she understood the way he checked her windows, the way he prowled the department seven hundred times a day to give some more rambunctious patients the stink eye. When Lyons was upset, he made sure everyone else was safe. His friend had died, and he hadn't been able to save her. And he had almost died.

That thought still made her eyes burn and ate through her ability to draw a full breath.

It was the same way she felt when she thought about Noelle, only mixed in with other feelings. The heart of it was the same choking desperation at the idea of losing him. She couldn't even imagine how it happened so fast. It was just over a week since she'd met him and suspected he might eviscerate the HR lady with his words.

Now she could barely stand the idea of not talking. Outside his pallor and the tic of his jaw, she had no idea what he was thinking.

Once he'd climbed in and buckled up, he still sat there with the keys in the ignition.

"Do you feel up to driving?" She did ask that, because she wasn't going to risk him in that way or make him feel forced to hold it together to keep her safe.

"I'm fine."

He wasn't fine.

"What are you thinking?"

"About the fastest way to The Roast."

Still a lie, but one that got coffee for her because she'd asked for it. Still taking care of her. If it helped him, she'd let him keep doing it.

"Do they have food too?"

* * *

Although he looked better by the time they'd finished their coffee, he hadn't wanted to speak about the hospital.

She knew how much it ate at him by his entire lack of speech, and by the kiss he gave her as they left The Roast, pressing her against the passenger side of the car.

He never spoke, but his kiss was a confession. He was shaken, but also angry with himself, with the situation? She didn't know. All she knew was that last night's slow, savoring kiss turned deep and demanding. Frigid winter winds blustered and blew against them, but the kiss stoked a fire within hot enough to bat back the cold. It took someone blowing a car horn right beside them to break them apart.

The drive back to her apartment was long and silent, convincing her that he'd just drop her off and take his leave.

But when they arrived, he parked and entered the building with her, still silent. As the door closed, Belle found herself pinned to it, his mouth on hers again, as if the hour between the Ramapo parking lot and her door had been a half-mile drive.

"I feel like I'm using you," he said, his mouth still against hers, hand cradling the back of her neck to keep her close, to get her closer.

"Using me?"

"Every time I feel too badly, I want to just drown it all out in your kisses."

"You didn't last night," she whispered, tugging his sweater up so she could get at the firm male flesh beneath. With the months that had definitely passed between last night and today, his bare flesh stirred a different feeling in her. She still wanted to protect him, but she mostly wanted closer. To feel his heat, heating her in return. She wanted to feel something *good*, and make him feel something good after a night and a day of shared suffering.

He let go of her, allowing the air to open up just long

enough for her to draw the material off his raised arms. She took the undershirt with it and spread her fingers over the muscled strength rippling under soft skin and the crisp, dark hair on his chest and tapering lower.

"No, last night I just wanted to hold you."

He did pause, needing to check the locks on the door they'd just passed through and locked back up, then began steering her back down the hallway to the bedroom they'd left this morning.

Belle had grown up in Arizona, her body adjusting to the heat over the course of a lifetime. December in New York, she survived the cold with layers.

He got her own sweater off and found the second sweater—a ribbed turtle neck. Once that was off, there was an undershirt.

"You're dressed like a Russian doll," he complained between kisses, but, once he got the long-sleeved shirt off, stepped back far enough that he wasn't even touching her anymore. He'd reached her bra, and he just looked, that frustration she'd heard diminishing in his eyes.

She felt his gaze in a tingling wake that had her body tightening and all her own patience evaporating, taking the rawness last night had exposed with it, or at least softened that year-old pain.

She wanted to be that for him, but his was even closer to the surface than hers. It felt fragile, like the tender first layer of skin over shredded tissue. Something to protect and nurture because even a touch could rip it open again.

This wasn't using her if she felt it too, if she wanted to give to him, to share with him, to be with him. The only place he touched her was the hand he'd taken when he stepped back, opening up the distance that kept her from reaching for him.

She croaked the question, mouth too dry for smoothness. "What are you doing?"

"Appreciating." The response was simple, but the look in his eyes deep with meaning. This wasn't simply lust or need.

"I haven't wanted in over a year. Not a hint of desire for anyone. The day I met you, there was a spark, and it's had a week to combust. I want to *see* you."

She might be quaking so hard her knees wanted to buckle, but she couldn't deprive him, not when it so clearly meant more than she'd have even had in her to hope for. But she wasn't strong enough to admit how much his words meant. It was all she could do to fumble open the closure on her jeans and shove them down. Helping. Just to provide what he needed. What *she* needed.

The corners of his mouth lifted as the material flopped around her ankles, pooling over her shoes.

"Can't wait?"

"In my head, it was a lot sexier." Her nervous, breathless laugh did nothing to add to the seduction. "Of course, that was last night, when I was going to show you the original set I'd picked."

She wobbled as she tried to toe the heels of her sneakers off and reached for him to keep from falling on her face. Not a smooth seduction. Probably not a seduction at all.

Except he took the hint and knelt down to help her, then stayed knelt low so that he got an entirely different, up-close inspection and perspective of her silky pink lace as his eyes locked to hers, and though she still saw amusement there—something she was actually thankful for after the past twenty-four hours—the stomach-clenching intent made her want to follow him down. An inch between them further than a mile. A look she'd have waited her whole life to see. He wanted her, and everything about the way he looked at her and touched her said he was *better* because he was with her. She had no doubt she felt better when she was with him. Even if it was only temporary.

"What were last night's like?"

"Red for extra sauciness." She smiled a little, then gave

in to the urge to brush her fingertips down his cheek. The first touch had him rising, hands coming to cup her face in return, bringing her mouth back to his, his kiss sweeter than the blistering need of moments before, but no less devastating.

"I like the pink," he said against her mouth, "but I want to see the red sometime…"

Sometime. In the future.

It wasn't a promise, just a request for *something* to continue between them. Not just today. Was it the start of something? She couldn't *have* forever, couldn't risk it, but maybe they could have something for *now*. And maybe *now* could last for a little while.

"When?"

"Christmas," he murmured. "Red for Christmas."

He wanted to spend Christmas with her. Her eyes stung, and she pressed against him, arms wrapping around his shoulders, relishing the mind-numbing wash of feeling that came when skin-to-skin with him. She'd choke on the hope filling her throat if he said anything else. Even knowing it couldn't last. Hope paid no mind to logic. This was only for now. For a little while longer.

His arms came around her and he lifted to move the few remaining feet to the bed, where he laid her down.

Every piece of clothing they removed tore away another burden that had pressed into her. And he felt it too. The intensity in his eyes when he looked at her didn't waver, but it did *brighten*. There was something so bright and hope-filled between them, it glowed like a thousand tiny lights. Or maybe a thousand tiny *candles*, which could be extinguished with a careless breath.

They burrowed into the still-tangled bedclothes, and he took his time—looking, touching, savoring—to the point her trembling became a second language, announcing what he did to her, and exactly how badly she wanted him to do that again.

It was a day of extremes. Sadness and worry to teasing and play, to the sexiest she'd ever felt.

By the time he'd reached his breaking point, she was almost mindless from his touch, from his deep, narcotic kisses, and it took him actually leaving the bed to paw through the bedside table to regain her senses enough for speech.

She rolled onto her side, the terrible, wonderful trembling in her body subsiding just enough for her to move. "Lyons?"

Lyons looked at her, her body a deep, gorgeous dusty rose, and shook his head. Too rushed, too drenched with need and frustration for speaking. He spotted the familiar shade of a bright blue box of condoms, grabbed it, bit into one corner and ripped the thing open to spill the shiny foil packets onto the bed.

Belle didn't say anything else, just tore one packet free and open, then reached for him. Her hands shook, which actually felt kind of amazing as she rolled it onto him. There was no grace in either of them in that moment, except when she met his eyes. He'd never seen anyone bestow serenity in a look. It was almost a religious experience, warming all the cold corners of his being he'd neglected too long. No matter how foolish, he wanted to worship.

When she'd settled it, the last piece of his patience shattered, and he followed her down onto the bed again.

A smart man would've urged her to turn over, taken her from behind so he couldn't fall into her eyes again. But he was an idiot. Or weak. Or a glutton for punishment. Like Wolfe, tempted to just let go and accept whatever price he had to pay to be with her. To stay here, in this small apartment, and have some peace.

He settled into the cradle of her thighs and held her gaze as he eased into her, a spike of pleasure already punching through his belly. Her eyes rolled back and closed. It had hit her too.

Starting to move, he found a rhythm that would ruin

him far too quickly, but need had taken over. When her eyes opened again, that connection—already too intense—surged, locked as surely as their bodies; even when they'd spiraled to a place where focus abandoned them, it remained, even deepened.

The first pulse of her climax finished him, and his jerking hips lost all semblance of control. But it was the sweetness that filled him, beamed straight into his chest from her eyes, that had him shaking long after he'd moved to her side and dragged her close.

She didn't ask him anything, not out loud, but with her head cradled on his chest, her eyes still on his face and him unable to look anywhere else, he still heard it.

"I'm all right," he whispered.

"You're still shaking."

And it had been a while.

He wouldn't deny it. Instead, he said, "I'm better than I've been in a long time."

And it was true. A feeling he could become addicted to.

"It's okay. This is scary." She misread him, but the way she said it—her eyes finally drifting away—he knew she was speaking to herself.

"Are you scared?"

She didn't answer immediately, but the worry he saw when she looked back was a megaphone. "Everyone I love dies."

The word quadrupled his pulse.

It wasn't an admission. It was too soon for that. Just an expression of fear, of what might happen if she *grew* to love him. Sex and intimacy, gateway drugs to love.

"Everyone dies. It has nothing to do with you." He touched her face, making her look him in the eye to make sure she'd heard him. "Noelle didn't die because you loved her."

He knew about guilt, how it could twist things.

When she nodded, when he was certain she'd heard him, he kissed her again and reached for another condom.

She didn't love him. This was comfort. And only until Christmas, until they'd both survived the most wonderful time of the year.

There had still been daylight when they'd reached the bedroom, but Lyons felt like a teenager—even after another, slower exploration of one another, and a pause to eat dinner, he'd made his dessert a feast of pleasure.

Now, at almost midnight, it was catching up with him.

"Your breathing is mighty slow and steady," Belle murmured, her arm wrapped over the arm he'd draped across her waist, then wiggling back against him a little more snugly.

He shifted to rest his cheek against the side of her neck, his chin touching her shoulder, unable to get any closer without rearranging her legs again. "I'm an old man."

She laughed. "You're, what? Thirty-five?"

"Thirty-seven."

"Oh, yep, you're a geezer now. The geezer-fication process begins at thirty-six."

"When you're relaxed, you get silly."

"When you're relaxed, you get Scottish."

"Do I?" He tried to remember the last thing he'd said before this.

"You said 'cannae.'" She tilted her head. "'I cannae go again yet.' Which was a lie too, because you did. But, just saying, you either get more Scottish when you're tired or when you're turned on. I'll need more research to figure out when."

"So, I'm a test subject now?"

"Afraid so."

"I suppose I'll submit, if it's in the name of science."

She laughed then, an unreserved belly laugh that jiggled his arm and his heart.

"I meant what I said. I want to spend Christmas with you and the red underwear, or all the lingerie you've got packed up."

"Good." She patted his arm and rolled to face him, settling down again when her lovely face was propped on the pillow in front of his. "Angel invited me to come upstate with her and Wolfe. I want you to come too."

Lyons groaned, closed his eyes and rolled to his back.

Angel. It had to have been Angel's invitation, all the time they'd been spending together.

"How about you stay with me at my place, and I'll even put up a tree and buy you something nice for all the gifts you gave. No shouting involved."

"Tempting." She made big eyes at him, clearly not even slightly tempted. "You don't have to shop. I'd just be happy to have you with me *there*."

"Ye fight dirty."

"Aye," she said, teasing him with just one word, but then grew far too sober. "You should spend Christmas with your family, Lyons. You don't know when you could lose him."

He sighed, the sentiment he'd been hearing and ignoring from his own conscience. "Fine, but I'm driving, not riding with them. I'm not eager to be trapped there if it gets miserable."

"You won't be miserable." She scooted back to him, following his change of position to prop her cheek on his chest. "Can we sleep now? This old guy I went to bed with exhausted me."

He felt himself grinning, but folded his arm over her shoulders to keep her close.

This wasn't a set-up. Just a normal request. Just a normal request from a girlfriend to spend time with him, and who'd lost too many people.

Sunday morning, he woke up with her watching him, her lovely features still soft from sleep, with that kind of bewildered expression she'd had for two mornings now, framed by wild, wavy, bed-mussed tresses. A vision he absolutely adored.

He could get used to waking like that.

"I want to go back to Ramapo," he said, because, after her, that was his second thought. And it set a little frown in her eyes.

"Again?"

"You don't have to come with me this morning." He leaned over to kiss away that little frown, but she pulled back.

The little frown deepened, a spark of anger lighting it. "You don't seriously think I'm going to be all right with that, do you?"

He'd hoped she wouldn't be all right with it but couldn't bring himself to ask it of her. She'd already given him so much this weekend. This week. Hell, she'd started giving to him the day after they'd met. Maybe the same day, depending on how he looked at it. He couldn't ask any more of her, even though it meant something to him to have her go too. She made him stronger.

"I thought I should give you an out."

"Well, that's nice and all, but I don't want an out." She didn't kiss him, but she did rise—gloriously naked—from the bed, making him regret having announced he wanted to go in the *morning*.

She didn't take time to make any fancy breakfast, just assembled toasted panettone, threw in some meats and cheese from Friday's antipasto, and made coffee.

They were on the road within an hour, and this time the drive flew by.

Parked on the roof again, because it was the last place he'd have parked when working there and that built in a kind of buffer that made it easier to go forward. He had to go forward. For some reason, he felt time ticking loudly this weekend as though, if he didn't get through this now, he'd lose his window. And his self-respect.

This time, when he stood with her little hand in his before the bank of elevators, he pressed the button.

There was still a knot in his belly, and it was possible that he might pass out if his pulse got any higher, but today was the day.

Although he didn't want to see worry on her face, once in the lift, he looked at her and saw her counting under her breath, in time with his pulse.

He looked down to where their hands joined and focused on where their fingers joined. She used hand-holding to monitor his vitals.

"I'm all right," he said, more to calm her than anything else.

It wasn't true. He was still on his feet and he didn't feel as if he was going to throw up the morning's breakfast, but he couldn't say for how long. At least he felt certain he'd have time to find a seat if the world started to go black around the edges.

"If you hit one-sixty and are still on your feet, expect to be tackled," she muttered, and he saw her check her watch and continue counting.

"What am I now?"

"One thirty-six."

He nodded, and through the front lobby of the hospital they went.

He'd never entered that way, not once while he worked there. Maybe that was why it was easier.

"One forty-five," she murmured as they stopped at the security station.

The guard, who'd worked there for at least ten years, laughed and stood up. "McKeag, you jerk, where have you been?"

Belle didn't want to let go of his hand, but Lyons squeezed

and pulled free, so he could hug the guard who rounded the station and gave him a back-slapping hug.

"Working in Manhattan." Lyons slapped back, and then returned to her. "Thought I'd swing by for a visit, but I don't have a badge anymore. I suppose protocol might've changed since I was here. Is it allowable to buzz us in?"

The guard's smile faltered at the oblique reference to how the man with the gun had gotten back to shoot him and Eleni, but Simms hadn't been the one to buzz him in, probably only because he'd been off for Christmas.

"Introduce me to your lady and I'll think about it," the guard said.

Being referred to as Lyons's lady gave Belle the sort of rush she suspected was something like the feeling people used drugs for—euphoric, thrilling, with a dash of pure terror. Still, she smiled, and it became wider when Lyons introduced her to the man called Simms and didn't correct that she wasn't his lady.

"They're busy back there. Might want to get some coffee before you go in," Simms added just as he buzzed the door.

Lyons's pulse, throbbing between her fingers, kicked back up as they walked into the department, but he *looked* better. There was none of the morning's grimness in his handsome face, and a much more subtle version of yesterday's pallor.

What she'd seen in Simms's reaction to Lyons's arrival was mirrored in the face of every single person in scrubs as they walked hand-in-heart-monitoring-hand into the bustling heart of the Ramapo emergency department.

When Lyons had worked at this hospital, he'd been different.

She didn't need these people to tell her that; all she had to do was compare the way they greeted him with the way he was received at Sutcliffe due to the way he behaved at Sutcliffe. She'd expected being shot had changed him; how could it not? But seeing how much…she'd never have predicted that.

More people hugged him, everyone gushed and patted his shoulder, and he always returned to her hand until a tall, reed-like man approached, looking dour.

This was it. She braced herself, sending a silent plea to Noelle for the courage and fire to shred this tall man with her words if he said the wrong thing.

"McKeag…" He didn't sound happy to see Lyons, but the pulse throbbing between her fingers slowed anyway. Not a sign he expected confrontation.

She swiveled her gaze from the tall doctor to Lyons and found him smiling again. "Nigel."

"You're late," Nigel said.

"Was I on the schedule?"

Lyons gave a tiny tug, and she stepped closer to him, focusing on the tall doctor even though it was Lyons's face she wanted to look at.

"You're actually still listed as having privileges," Nigel said, half shrugging as if it didn't matter at all, but the slow slide of his gaze to her said he was measuring—either his own reaction or whether she changed the equation.

She smiled, although it was given she had no idea what was going on.

"Who is this?"

"Ysabelle Sabetta." Lyons used her whole name. "She's a nurse practitioner. And, Belle, this jerk is Nigel Benet."

Nigel offered a hand and an explanation. "Former best friend."

For the first time, Lyons's smile faltered. "Nigel—"

"Do you have time to see a couple patients?" he interrupted. "I'm serious. We're stacking them like sardines—flu and bronchitis running rampant this December. You won't be paid for it, but it would go a distance to keeping your friends glad to see you after a year of unreturned calls and texts."

Lyons hesitated, shifting his gaze to her. She could see he wanted to. And it seemed like such a positive turn compared to yesterday's aborted visit, all she could do was nod.

"Nige?" Lyons called, because Nigel had already moved on, wherever he'd been going. "Your office the same?"

"Yep."

"Belle's going to take a load off there."

"Sure."

The man stepped into a room, and Lyons guided her through the department to a small office in the back, turned the lights on and found a small, portable heater under the desk. One he knew was there, because he knew his friend's office would be cold.

"Are you sure you're all right with this? I'll try to keep it short. An hour or so? Do you have anything to read?"

"Don't worry about me." Within the safe, private confines of the office, she kissed him quickly and asked, "Are you sure you're okay with it?"

He looked as astonished by his reaction as she was. "I… expected my heart might explode before we got in the door, but it was better… It was all right. I'm all right."

There were little pauses between every statement, as if he was taking some internal inventory of his vitals before he committed to the words.

"I'll read my field guide, then." She pulled the phone from her pocket—he'd returned it to her that morning before they left—and sat down in front of the heater.

"Three doors down is a break room, if you're looking for the world's worst coffee."

"I'll wait for The Roast."

He plowed into a cabinet on the door, pulled out a still-boxed stethoscope, found a notepad and pen in another drawer, and went out to it.

This man who smiled, who people *loved*, was so different from the Lyons she'd known, it was as if she'd just met a stranger. But then, she'd actually seen glimpses of him here and there.

Should she be relieved, or worried that, now he'd gotten over this hump in his recovery, he'd be done with her?

Her heart squeezed, and although she knew it would hurt, she didn't think it would destroy her.

She'd lost everyone she loved because they'd *died*. If she had to lose him, maybe it could just be because he left this time?

Then she could know he was still out there, and hope he was happy.

Be glad he survived her.

That would be better. She could survive that.

CHAPTER TWELVE

LYONS FOUND NIGEL leaving a patient's room and got his directives.

It was a little harder to walk into the treatment rooms—and he was quietly relieved that the room where he and Eleni had been shot wasn't one he'd been assigned.

Nigel had either given him the new doctor cases, or he was serious when he said they were overflowing with flu and bronchitis, because he had exactly one of each before they met up again in the corridor.

"Your neck got thicker," Nigel said, a nod to their old manner of ribbing.

"I took therapy to the next level." He hadn't ever been lax with his fitness, but since the shooting he'd put on a good thirty pounds of muscle, while his friend remained rail-thin. "It comes in handy sometimes in the ER."

"Does it?" Nigel looked at him a little longer. "Ysabelle probably doesn't mind it."

"If she does, she hasn't said anything." Lyons could see new lines on his friend's face, noted the thinner hair, but he couldn't return fire, not when he was so deep in the red.

Besides, they were circling the subject of his changes since he'd last been there because of how he'd been before. And it stared him in the face just how wrong it had been to cut Nigel, of all these friends, out of his life after the shooting.

It was a harsher version of what he'd done with Wolfe, or maybe gentler. He still spoke to his brother. Kind of. He still saw him, but any camaraderie they should've had was gone, but then they'd never had the kind of closeness Belle had enjoyed with her sister. They'd both grown up guarding their words, protecting their vulnerable spots from everyone, especially family.

Since the shooting, Wolfe had been trying to change things; Lyons was the one blunting it now.

"I'm sorry I disappeared," he said abruptly.

Nigel gave a slow nod. "I get it. I'm really surprised to see you here. I don't know if I could've come back."

"Because she died?" he asked, not really wanting to hear the answer.

Nigel gave him an odd look. "Because you almost died too. I'm still not sure how you survived."

"Me either." He'd seen the files and imaging records. "Maybe I shouldn't have. But I did, and hate being reminded of how close it came."

Nigel glanced across the main floor toward his office, and back to Lyons. "She the woman who's finally getting you to turn your back on your heartless bachelor ways?"

Yes.

He heard the word bouncing through his whole body but didn't say it. He wasn't ready to say it. And if he ever got ready, it should be to her first.

"Maybe." The answer lacked volume, but it still rang in his ears.

Nigel slapped him on the back again. "Well, better get her before she gets bored with your thick neck and looks for a man with a long, delicate, flamingo-pink neck and oversized, hyper-masculine Adam's apple."

Lyons laughed despite himself as Nigel described his own neck, ribbing himself since Lyons hadn't. "She's angling for a trip to The Roast."

"She's a keeper, then."

Lyons could only nod, his chest as full of gratitude as it had been full of mud earlier.

"If you want to come back, I'll see to it. Otherwise, I think your privileges expire mid-year. Just to keep in mind."

Lyons nodded again but couldn't really get his mind around the offer. "Thank you. It was good to see you."

"Send me an invitation to the wedding. I'll keep my schedule open."

Now Nigel was just messing with him, but he still smiled.

A few minutes later, he knocked on the office door out of habit, and stepped in.

Whatever she'd said about spending her time reading, she was doing anything but. Her phone sat on the desk, and she sat across the room on the small loveseat.

"Everything okay?" she asked, scooting to the edge of the leather seat to stand as soon as he came in.

"It is. Is your phone grounded?"

"I almost emailed Noelle, so I thought I better put it over there."

"Did you have a picture to send?" He couldn't imagine what kind of picture she'd have gotten in that dismal little office.

"Just wanted to talk," she whispered, and in the next moment she was pressed against him, her arms around his shoulders. "But you're okay?"

She'd wanted to talk. He should ask what about, but he needed a little time first.

He might not be good yet, it was all too tricky and barbed. "I'm better than I have been for a long time."

She stayed against him and he wrapped his arms as fully around her as he could, overlapping to the point he almost touched his own ribs.

"Where is she buried?" he asked, into her hair. He hadn't ever asked because the subject seemed so fraught.

"Arizona."

"Where you're from?"

She nodded.

"Maybe after Christmas, you should go visit." He couldn't have suggested that even a day ago, but today he could, and went further. "I'll go with you, if you like?"

"Maybe," she whispered.

Not ready yet, and maybe it wouldn't be so bad for her to keep emailing her sister if she felt the need to talk. It wasn't that much different from pouring your heart out at a grave site.

Except that it let her pretend everything was normal, that her sister was somewhere, reading whatever she sent.

"We should go get some coffee and go home. I need to pack a weekend bag. You need to pack too."

She leaned back then, her arms still around him, and despite the sadness she still struggled with, she smiled at him. "Are you going to sleep at my apartment tonight?"

"If you don't mind." He squeezed her. "After I pack my bag."

And he needed an excuse for the time it would take to get a gift for her before tomorrow.

Belle had never been to the Catskills, but Lyons had made it inevitable that she would fall asleep by making sure she hadn't slept much last night.

He'd been different since they'd visited the hospital. Even when they'd gone to bed, he'd been different. More deliberate and present, full of deep, meaningful gazes and whispered words.

It felt so much like love, she'd given in to it. There was nothing to be done but accept that if she'd wanted to avoid loving again, she should've done things differently from the outset. Once you loved someone, and once they loved you—she was almost certain he did—there was no considering turning that love away.

Even if she thought she should for his own good, it was too late. Even if she left, even if she took that misery and ran, she'd still love him. Working that out, he would still be in danger, if she was as cursed as that small, superstitious voice in her head liked to tell her.

"He said it was a cabin," she said as the massive cabin-like mansion came into view. "I don't think this is it."

"This is it," Lyons countered, sounding certain.

"That's got to be a bed and breakfast, or maybe a hunting lodge for the Rockefellers."

"This is it," he reiterated, nodding to one side of the equally insanely big barn, where garages had been installed, and where Wolfe was currently walking out of the nearest bay.

He waved, then gestured toward the cabin. If it could be called a cabin.

Angel came out to meet them, and the four of them unloaded the car, each grabbing some of the few bags and gifts they'd brought.

The door opened directly into a massive room, with towering ceilings, open timber-frame construction, and second-, possibly third-floor areas wrapping around three sides.

In the center of the room sat a Christmas tree—massive, fresh and which Angel had obviously been decorating. "We came up yesterday to try and get it all sorted out before you guys got here, but we got distracted."

The hesitation and shyness of her confession had Belle's cheeks burning in sympathy. "Well, I love to decorate a tree. Let's do this."

Lyons and Wolfe clanged into the main room, then headed up one set of stairs to the right side of the balcony.

"There are a bunch of rooms up there. If they pick one you don't like, pick another. In fact, you could probably sleep in a different room every night if you wanted."

The way Angel said it gave a good hint at her still acclimating to this lifestyle. All Belle had experienced of it before was Lyons's fancy car, and the knowledge that he had an apartment on Park, which she hadn't yet visited. "Where does Wolfe live?"

"We live together."

"But where? On Park too?"

"Tribeca." Angel helped her out of her coat, and then tossed another log onto the fire. "In an old converted church. You should come for dinner. Lyons has said he'll come after Christmas."

Just then, Lyons and Wolfe appeared on the stairs and, although Lyons smiled at her, Wolfe was the one calling to Angel. "We're going to go for a quick ride."

"Okay," Angel called back and picked up a box of ornaments to hand to Belle. "Horses," Angel explained, since the men were gone. "Wolfe wants to talk to him about some things."

Lyons followed Wolfe into the barn. The two aspects of this holiday he'd managed to build excitement for was spending time with Belle and riding the horses he'd been promised.

The idea of spending time with his brother, while something he wanted to improve on, he still didn't know how to do it, and that carried tension down his spine, future disappointment on the horizon that would be his doing. But the fresh scent of sweet hay and the line of sleek noses and intelligent eyes popping over the horse stalls at the sound of their approach helped ease that.

"I have an ulterior motive for asking you to go for a ride," Wolfe announced as they entered the other side of the barn, wrecking the harmonious mood adjustment horses always brought him.

"I thought you might." Lyons took a deep breath, closed the door and approached the nearest stall, offering his hand to the horse to scent as he settled in for the rough conversation he felt coming. "About Angel?"

"I think that's the first time I've heard you call her by name."

"Belle is insistent," Lyons said, stroking the pretty bay roan, forehead to muzzle.

Wolfe's dramatically wide smile was made for smacking, but Lyons resisted. "Tell me what you wanted to tell."

"I asked her to marry me," Wolfe responded, his smile gone when Lyons glanced back.

"I know." Lyons wasn't sure when he'd figured it out—Angel didn't wear a ring—but probably about the time she'd moved in. "When?"

"This summer," Wolfe answered in as few words as possible, which didn't exactly invite conversation, which was on par for the way they usually communicated. Something about the way he stood, hands shoved into pockets, shoulders up around his ears, said there was more to it.

"Congratulations," Lyons said by rote, and even kind of meant it. It wasn't so much that he was suddenly pro-marriage, but he'd recently come to understand how it was to find someone who made life easier. At least for now.

"I hope it's a marriage completely unlike our parents'," he added, and sincerely meant that one.

Those words made Wolfe flinch, his expression turning sheepish as he pulled his hands free and scrubbed both over his face. "About them…"

It was Lyons's turn to flinch. "Tell me you didn't call them."

"I didn't call them," Wolfe repeated, then screwed it all up by adding, "but I'm going to."

This was what came from Lyons holding his gullible little brother at arm's length, him making terrible mistakes. No more. If Wolfe ever needed to hear it straight, it was now. "Why the devil would you want to do that?"

"Because she should know what she's getting into, marrying me. She knows you, she likes you, despite the fact that you've turned into someone who growls and shouts at everyone. For perfectly good reasons, I know that, but she needs to see the slow-motion horror show they are before she's tied to them too."

Lyons heard the complaint about himself in there but pushed past it for the important parts: the horror show and how Angel would react to them when Lyons was bad enough.

The investigator he'd hired to find out about Angel when Wolfe had admitted dating her flashed back to his mind.

"What about her family?"

"We'll go see them too, though in a controlled environment. She doesn't want them to know where she lives."

No doubt.

"So, what is it you want from me? Permission? Because you're a grown man. I can't protect you from life anymore. Or them."

"I'm not asking you to protect me. I'm telling you that I'm going to see them, and I wanted to know if you wanted them to come here, or if you'd rather we go there."

"Go there," Lyons said without hesitation, although he felt his blood pressure rising. "Don't bring them into your life. If you feel you must introduce them, don't let them into your home. God, Wolfe. Don't let them into your life. If you don't let them into your life, they shouldn't matter to her, if she—"

"They *don't* matter to her," Wolfe said, cutting in. "What matters to her is her own family, which have held her down her whole life, and you don't even know the half of that. We have their reputations transferred to us, I know, but their reputations were that of being immoral, and scandal-ridden, and if you dug into her background, you know who her people are. You *warned* me who they are, like you don't remember us undeservedly carrying the taint they'd built."

"I'm warning you fresh because you *don't* know who our parents are. Not really. You don't know the lengths they went to in order to get back at one another. You don't know because I shielded you from it." Lyons heard his voice bouncing off the walls, and the horses began making noise in their stalls, agitated, upset.

Wolfe joined him looking toward the animals and lowered his voice. "What are you talking about?"

"I'm saying that so long as I did her dirty work, she did not ask you."

"Mother?"

Lyons nodded once.

"What dirty work?"

He sucked in a breath and began to pace, because in that second, with the jumble of thoughts in his head, he needed to move.

He *wanted* to go back to Belle, and let her make him feel good again, and then he remembered that same feeling with his mother. She paid attention only when he did what she demanded, and that attention was worth more than the pain he went through to do whatever…usually to their father.

"Lyons."

"I dropped off letters to the papers, which she'd written to stack the deck. It didn't matter if he was in the wrong or she was, she always went for the underhanded play, and usually I was her mule," Lyons said, starting small.

"So, she called the media down on us?"

Lyons nodded.

"What else?"

"I got pictures of Father with his mistresses. Once I got way more intimate photos than I should've ever gotten. The next time, when I refused, she sent you away to school as my punishment."

Wolfe's mouth fell open. "When I was little?"

Lyons nodded. It was only for half a year that time, but it was motivating. "After that, I did get pictures of him with his mistresses going or coming from a room alone. But she brought you home. You were a pawn, you were miserable. You called me all the time, crying to come home."

Wolfe nodded again, but he was now pacing. And suddenly paced right on out of the barn. Lyons hadn't even gotten to the moral: people were users. They treated you the way that benefited them.

Even Belle. He excused it because he wanted her, and he sympathized, but she'd given gifts to him because she was trying to survive Christmas alone. He got that, but she'd had a motive.

And he had a motive for being with her: she made him feel better. He wasn't sure it was about attraction, or that she gave him the opportunity to protect her as he'd failed to do with Eleni. They had broken hearts tying them together and might have nothing else in common if they didn't have trauma, and need, and sex to bind them.

He stayed with the horses, letting Wolfe muddle through it on his own.

He needed a ride. It had been far too long, and it always cleared his head.

CHAPTER THIRTEEN

THEY'D HUNG THE ornaments on the tree and were working on fashioning a bow out of an oversized roll of sheer, glittery ribbon when Wolfe returned from the barn alone.

Both Angel and Belle turned to see him enter, and although it looked as if he'd intended to keep plowing through, he paused and said, "Lyons decided to go for a ride."

"I thought you were going to ride too," Angel said, and Wolfe didn't answer audibly, but the one arm flying into the air and his headshake said enough.

He and Lyons didn't want to ride together, for *reasons*. And since Wolfe had wanted to talk to Lyons about something, the reasons might be legit, not just Lyons having a moment.

He disappeared down a downstairs hallway.

"I'm going to go see what happened." Angel looked at the ribbon and ornaments they'd been decorating with. "Do you need help? If you need help, just give me a few minutes."

"I can make the bow. Don't worry." She waited for Angel to be out of the room and abandoned the ribbon to look out of the massive front windows. The barn and paddock were in easy view, and she didn't see Lyons.

Maybe she should go check.

Or she could call him. Or text.

Goodness, he'd been in such a good mood yesterday. Sure, he'd been different after his visit to the hospital, but she still hoped it'd all shake out. That he'd find his new normal, embrace the way he felt now and become again the old Lyons she'd met yesterday.

Not comforted.

Was this a Christmas thing?

Oh, hell, it was *Christmas Eve*, and she'd known that all day but still hadn't put it together with what he was feeling. She'd just been worried about *them*, about how much longer there would *be* a them. If he'd want her when he found his new normal.

She hadn't even realized, let alone asked, how he was doing on the actual anniversary of the shooting. God, she sucked.

She should've declined Angel's invitation and stayed home with him, which had been what Lyons had wanted. He'd only come north with her because she wanted him to spend time with his brother. To make her happy, and now they were fighting.

It only took a moment to retrieve her coat, but no sooner had she opened the door than he rode out of the barn and into the paddock. She dithered. He liked horses, maybe a ride would help.

She shed her coat again to give him time. What was she going to do, chase his horse and yell so he heard her?

If he didn't come back soon, she'd check on him. It was almost dark. He couldn't be out there too long.

Or if Angel came back, looking worried or with bad news, she'd reevaluate.

Finish the bow, keep busy, that was how life worked for her.

She had it made and was fluffing the loops to the fullest when Angel returned.

"I don't think either of us can reach the top of the tree without climbing on something." Her southern accent was stronger, and her eyes pink when Belle looked at her.

"Did they have a doozy?"

Angel shook her head. "Must've. He won't say. He talks to me about everything now, but he said he needs some time with it, whatever that means."

Belle fell back on her usual coping mechanisms. Helping others helped her. "How about we have some tea, wait for them to calm down and talk about the wedding?"

Angel hadn't yet mentioned it, but Belle had seen the gorgeous diamond glittering on her finger first thing.

She followed Belle's gaze to her hand, and her expression softened. "We decided it was time to wear it since he was going to tell Lyons today."

Was that what had sparked the fight?

She wouldn't ask. Angel didn't need to hear that kind of negativity.

Belle rounded the leather ottoman she'd been using as a seat to keep from glittering up the *cloth* furniture, dropped the bow and went to hug her. "It's beautiful. You'll be a gorgeous bride, and in fifty years this'll just be a funny story that only got funny in hindsight. Now, let's have tea, and you can tell me your wedding ideas until the boys return to their senses."

She faked chipper pretty well, because it helped her to take care of other people. If she didn't have that, even if she was using Angel, she would sit, and her thoughts would spiral, and everything would feel so much worse. At least this way, she might be able to help Angel feel better and that helped her too.

Tea and wedding talk was a good idea, but nearly impossible to pull off. Every word dripped with effort, and quickly rolled around to Lyons and Wolfe again.

If Belle couldn't talk to Noelle, she needed to find someone she *could* talk to. The time she'd spent with Lyons had proven that to her. And if it hadn't, seeing him reunited with his old friends from work would've. Life was scary—people could be killed or die from disease without warning—but it wasn't worth the effort alone. It wasn't up to her to decide for others if she was worth the risk of being around, it was on her to make herself worth the risk. Do the most good she could.

"We went to his old hospital in Ramapo," Belle said during a pause. "He was a completely different person."

Angel angled her chair toward Belle. "Wolfe said that after the shooting he changed. Drastically."

Which still fell short of explaining the difference she'd seen.

"He smiled, without me saying something silly to him. He smiles for me sometimes, but they're prompted by something. But there? It was probably easier." Her throat closed and the burning in her eyes made her take a moment. "It's what I think it must have been like for someone to meet my sister and then meet me. We looked exactly alike but had completely different personalities."

"Had?" Angel's question came softly, and Belle remembered telling Angel she sent photos to her sister, and that pit in her stomach churned again.

"Noelle…"

Died.

Noelle died.

Noelle passed away.

All the ways she could say it, but her mouth still refused the words. Instead, she said, "MRSA, last year. I haven't quite figured out how to accept it. I'm trying."

Angel's eyes grew damp, mirroring her own, and she nodded rather than saying words. A show of support she was thankful for, acknowledged and felt without deepening the pain, but it still took her a moment to get back to words.

"At Ramapo, it was like discovering he was a twin, except for when he looked at me. When he looked at me, I still saw *him*. I can't explain."

"I think I understand." Angel refilled the teacups, not forcing the words, letting them dribble out as they came.

"But this was part of why you started giving him the gifts, right? You wanted to change him?"

Angel's wording stopped her, forced her to consider her gifting goals.

She hadn't known that Lyons would become entirely different, but yes, she'd hoped that he'd become happier and that, by extension, would change him or his behavior. Make him into who he was *supposed* to be, or who he'd been before whatever had happened to him—she hadn't known at the time what had happened or how drastic.

"I hope it works," she said finally.

"I think it is," Angel said, then stopped, gaze focused over Belle's shoulder.

"You hope what works?" Lyons's voice came from behind her and sent her heart pounding. From surprise, she rationalized, as he'd only caught her saying things he already knew.

But having your quasi-boyfriend stumble over you talking about him when he'd just quarreled with his brother? Reason to be nervous.

She tried to act normal, rising to greet him. "Hey, is everything okay?"

His arms were crossed, and his eyes had steeled, grown as cold as they had been when he'd stared down the hockey player.

"I asked you a question. You hope *what* works?" His voice was almost one tone, low and precisely spoken. He yelled when he was angry, but when he got really quiet, it was time to worry.

She replayed their conversation in her head, and, based on when Angel had gone quiet, it hadn't been long he'd been there. He'd only caught the end. But taken out of context *You wanted to change him* and *I hope it works* sounded mercenary, or at the very least manipulative.

She rounded the table to get closer, wind this back before it got out of control. If she could touch him, he'd feel it;

he always felt it. Maybe touch could get through whatever this anger was about, the remnants of his fight with Wolfe?

Phrase it better.

"I hoped the gifts and connection to someone would help you feel happier." At a foot or so away, she reached for him, but he stepped back from her.

"That's not what you meant." He spoke through clenched teeth. "'I hope it works' means you had a *plan*. And you're comfortable enough that I'm falling for it to openly discuss it where I might hear you."

This wasn't just anger with Wolfe spilling over. What else was it?

She froze where she stood, not wanting to exacerbate the situation. He'd been in a good mood from when they'd woken up, throughout the long drive, and even when he and Wolfe had gone to ride. Now, his teeth gritted, he was struggling to contain himself. That was more than simple anger.

"What happened in the barn?" she asked, the conversation landscape shifting sands.

"That's not an answer."

"Lyons, you came in at the tail end of a conversation," Angel said, trying to help. "We were talking about how she wanted to help you feel happier with the gifts."

"Stay out of this, Conley," he shouted, suddenly, which seemed like a step down in his anger. Anger meant shouting; rage was quiet. "Unless you two *are* partners in some marriage and money scheme."

His voice must have carried, because before either Belle or Angel could respond, Wolfe's door slammed, and his running feet stayed the conversation.

In only a moment, he was there. "What's going on?"

"Your girlfriend and Sabetta have a scheme going on. I told you. I *told* you. No one is that selfless. You're just love-blind and can't see what's right in front of you. I should've just let Mother have at you, maybe it would've opened your damned eyes."

Wolfe looked at Angel, his expression showing his conflict, placed in the middle.

Angel gave an almost imperceptible shake of her head, and the tiniest shrug. The very next second, Wolfe was at her side. And Belle couldn't miss the difference between their relationships.

Wolfe and Angel stuck together, but Lyons didn't even want her *touching* him. A tiny shake of Angel's head was enough for Wolfe to rally to her side.

Lyons didn't trust her at all, and it couldn't be all about that snippet of conversation. What else had she done?

"Maybe we should talk about this later, when you've had a minute…" It was the last tactic she had to defuse the situation.

"Plotting, scheming, faking feelings, did you make up Noelle too?"

His words dropped like an anvil through her insides, plowing warmth and tender feelings right out of her.

"Make up Noelle?" she repeated, but saying the words didn't make sense of them.

The flick of his eyebrows challenged her, dared her to deny it, as if he *had* just scored some win against her.

The incredulity she'd felt faded, and the hollow place left in her chest filled with fire, and her palm began to burn as if she'd just slapped him. She *wanted* to slap him.

"What did you just say to me?" she shouted, launching forward to slam her palms into his shoulders, shoving roughly. Everything that might have happened today didn't matter, she'd just run out of a willingness to bend or give him the benefit of the doubt, when he could say *that* to her.

For some reason, he didn't shout back. He also didn't move away, outside the half step back her shove demanded. He just watched her with that cold indifference that drove her over the edge. He had everything, and he didn't care. Wolfe. Angel. *Her.* He didn't love any of them. He used her sister as a weapon to hurt her, and it *did.*

But the fury she'd prayed for Noelle to send her yesterday finally came. And tears. And screaming.

He wanted to use Noelle's death to hurt her? She'd let him see it.

"She was *everything* to me and I *lost* her. I'd do anything to have her back, including whatever you think this is. All I've been doing is trying to show you love, but you're dead inside. You don't have many people who love you, and you should know better than anyone how fleeting life is. You could lose *him* tomorrow." She jabbed her finger in Wolfe's direction. "But you still don't even *try* to be a brother to him."

Wolfe and Angel were quiet, ghosts haunting the kitchen. Not that they could say anything that would matter to Lyons or stop her.

This man who she thought she loved, who she'd been fighting for, thought so little of her that in a moment of paranoia he didn't even hesitate to use the biggest weapon she'd given him.

She shoved at his chest again, as hard as she could, his silence screaming back at her.

"Say something! Why don't you ask Wolfe what it's like to hear your brother might die?"

She shoved again, plowing him backward, step by step, into the great room.

"Ask him what it's like to *live* for the low, regular beeps of the heart monitor. To be afraid to blink because if you look away, it might stop."

Another shove, but it didn't help. It wasn't helping, it wasn't enough.

"Give up sleeping, and eating, and bathing for over a week while your sister is dying because no one, especially not *her*, should die alone."

"Belle…" He finally spoke, his voice soft, not just quiet, and through her water-filled eyes he looked *shocked*.

She shoved again, he staggered back, several steps this time, and out of her way.

"You know what I want from you? Nothing. I want nothing from you." She let it out, too far gone to care. "I was wrong and stupid to hope—it's too late for you."

He didn't say anything else, and she was out of words too.

Back toward the kitchen, Wolfe and Angel hovered. "What room did he pick? Where's my bag?"

Her voice rasped, her throat raw, and all strength just gone.

"Upstairs. First on the right," Wolfe answered, giving her a destination for the *out* she desperately needed.

Belle took the stairs as quickly as she could, making a point not to look at Lyons.

She heard Angel say something behind her but couldn't make out words above the blood rushing in her ears. When she reached the upper floor, Angel was beside her and took Belle's hand, offering silent support and leading her to the right room.

"I can't stay," Belle croaked as they stepped inside. "I'm sorry. We're ruining your Christmas. I can't stay."

Angel grabbed Belle in a quick, hard hug. "Don't apologize. And don't worry about us. This was always a worry with Lyons."

Because he had so much rage in him even toward her, and she didn't know why.

"I'll take you wherever you want to go," Angel said. "Or kick Lyons out."

"I'll go." Belle grabbed her bag and swung the strap onto her shoulder, leaving the gifts. She was already crying—much more sympathy would make her fragile internal supports buckle. "Train station? Bus? Airport? I don't care. Whatever is closest. I just can't be here anymore."

* * *

Lyons watched Belle hurtle past him and up the stairs, tears pouring over her cheeks.

The places where her palms had slammed into his chest burned like fresh brands.

She was leaving. Not fighting to stay. None of that had been arguing to stay.

"Come on," Wolfe said, stepping into his line of sight, and urging him to move. "Let's have a drink. Don't just stand and watch her go."

He listened hard, but whatever she was doing upstairs was quiet. He couldn't hear moving or talking. But she wouldn't have to do much to get ready to go. They hadn't been there long enough to unpack.

"Is she going?" he asked Wolfe because it didn't seem true, or make much sense. If she was scheming to marry money, wouldn't she be trying to make up?

His chest burned.

"Angel's taking her wherever she wants to go," Wolfe said, then actually nudged him, still speaking gently. "Come on, man, don't make her walk past you."

Because she was leaving.

And him standing there, forcing her to go past him to get out, would be another jerk move... That was what Wolfe's tone said.

He gave in to the nudging and walked back to where all this started. Half-filled cups of tea and a plate of biscuits sat on the table. Lyons sat too, but everything was in slow motion. Even his thoughts didn't come to him without effort. Without pauses.

Because she was leaving. Because of what he'd said.

Why had he said that?

Wolfe joined him, placing two tumblers on the table and opening a fresh bottle of whiskey.

From the other room, he heard the front door open and close, and stood up.

Wolfe stood too, laying a hand on his shoulder to still him.

"Don't." He spoke too gently, with too much sympathy. "She needs time, at least."

"You think she'll return?" Lyons sat again but kept watching his little brother's sad face. "No. You don't."

"I don't," Wolfe confirmed. "But if there's any chance, it isn't now. She won't be able to hear anything but what you said."

"I don't know why I said that," Lyons mumbled, and the drink suddenly looked very good. Very necessary. He drained his glass in one and looked back to Wolfe, who wasn't looking back at him in return. Just frowning into his drink. Sad. He was sad.

For *him*. For what Lyons had just lost.

She'd said he was too far gone. There was no love in him. That wasn't true. If that was true, he wouldn't feel acid searing his insides.

Why had he said that?

Because he thought she was lying. Had tricked him. Didn't truly feel for him, and he wanted her to feel something real.

Because he couldn't hear the wrongness of it before giving it voice.

God, was he really that big an ass?

Yes.

Ask Wolfe what it's like to hear your brother might die.

He was the kind of ass who never thought to ask Wolfe what it was like for him when he was shot. What it was like as a surgeon, to wait for his brother's trauma surgery, knowing too well all the things that could go wrong.

How would he feel if Wolfe were in his ER, life hanging on the skills of another doctor?

Hell.

If he was that selfish, he owed it to her—and to Wolfe—to ask. To talk to him.

Then she might be able to forgive him.

CHAPTER FOURTEEN

ON CHRISTMAS EVE Angel had driven Belle to the nearest railway station to get her back to her apartment.

On Christmas Day, Belle had boarded a plane at La Guardia to take her broken, battered heart home, to Scottsdale.

Although Angel had made sure she understood she still had friends and the support of both her and Wolfe, this was something she needed her sister to help pick up the pieces.

Losing Lyons before she'd dealt with losing her sister had been the event that had forced her to face reality. Reality was she hadn't grieved, she'd run. It was time to stop running, even if that meant her job wouldn't wait for her return.

Christmas Day travel was rougher than she'd have expected—airports still clogged with people, inclement weather delaying flights and forcing alternative routes. She saw Atlanta before getting stuck in Chicago for a day until a storm passed. She didn't make it to Phoenix until late afternoon, the day after Christmas, to pick up her rental car.

Despite the late hour on a winter's day, she made it to the cemetery and located Noelle's grave a short distance from Nanna and Dad's, catching her first sight from a distance of the gravestone she'd bought but fled the state before seeing placed.

Seeing her sister's name, their shared birthday and the date of Noelle's death engraved in the polished stone made roots sprout from her feet.

The stone faced the east, and the sun crept lower on the horizon behind it, casting long shadows from the head-stones, but, at three graves away, Belle couldn't make herself approach.

Like Lyons on the first trip to Ramapo, she'd come ninety-five percent of the way, but didn't have the strength or the will to carry her the last few yards to her destination.

She shoved the thought aside. The last thing she wanted was to have something else in common with him. But that was what had taken her away from Noelle the past eighteen months, putting painful subjects out of her mind because she wasn't ready to deal.

She really wasn't ready to deal with Lyons. There was an argument to be made about dealing with one emotionally devastating thing at a time, and not tainting all the emotions tied to the loss of her sister with the loss of *him*, but Noelle was who she would've gone to over her breakup with Lyons.

So, this was it. She had to deal.

Tomorrow.

She'd start talking tomorrow, when the sun had risen and she could feel new light, and maybe some hope for the future with it. Now, the last sliver of the sun could be seen above the flat horizon, and the long shadow from Noelle's stone reached out, stretching over the distance to touch the toe of her left shoe. Reaching out.

That was what she had now, a shadow for a sister, and a shredded heart she needed help mending.

"I'll come back tomorrow." She whispered the promise to her feet and fled back to her car to find her hotel and sleep.

The twenty-seventh of December, she woke to texts from Angel, and it helped ground her to what was current in her reality. That she had a life back in New York to return to once she'd sorted herself out.

She arrived early, with the dew still on the grass, and set about tending the grave. The mowers kept the grass trimmed, but no one came with an edging tool to clean up around the stone. She'd brought scissors for that.

She'd also brought lilies and water, which she placed in the little vase on the base of the stone. Making it prettier. Doing things, anything, that would let her have an external focus. Not talking. She couldn't even think of what to say, her heart too raw for words.

When she'd done all she could, she sat in the grass, leaned against the stone and pulled out her phone, her point of connection to her sister for the last eighteen months. Bypassing the email, she opened Photos.

Only when the day was half gone did she open the email client and begin to read aloud, starting the first day, when she'd still been emailing with the notion that her sister was gone and would never read it. It wasn't even a week later that the emails became more an exercise in self-deceit, speaking to Noelle as if she were reading them. Comforting herself with lies.

When the sun went down, she returned to the hotel, numb and exhausted, vowing to bring more tissues tomorrow, and more water.

Her second full day in Scottsdale—second day actually grieving for her sister. When she got there the sun had already been in the sky long enough to dry the grass. She wound the little red gas-saving rental down an access road that would put her nearer to Noelle's grave, and parked. Today she had daisies; the prospect of sitting with dead flowers just made it all seem that much worse.

She parked for the shortest walk, and that meant she approached it from behind, but when she rounded the stone she found a fresh bunch of white roses, wrapped in tissue paper, lying on the ground.

Despite her having not visited the grave for over a year, when she'd come yesterday, there had been no signs anyone else had ever visited or left flowers. It was possible anything left might have been cleared away, but she couldn't think of anyone who would bring Noelle a bunch of roses.

She took a moment to remove yesterday's lilies from the little vase beside the stone, poured in some extra water and settled today's daisies within. Only then did she pick up the flowers to look for a card, or anything that might let her know where they'd come from. Was it possible a florist delivered to the wrong grave? They'd wither today, lying in the heat.

When she found nothing to tell her who sent them, she unwrapped the blossoms and wove the long-stemmed white buds into the vase with her daisies, finally speaking to Noelle without the aid of the script, pre-written months ago.

"Maybe Angel and Wolfe sent these. I didn't tell them which Scottsdale cemetery, but maybe they used those private investigators *he* told me about to find out where you were and sent flowers, so we'd know they were thinking of us."

So unnatural, speaking to the air. Much more unnatural than sending emails had felt. With the emails, it was just like when she'd emailed Noelle in life. Out loud, she couldn't pretend she wasn't speaking to a stone.

Noelle had been the talker of the two of them. Belle had always participated, but never been so animated and entertaining as her sister. Probably a reason why she needed to keep up with the talking.

"They've been kind and supportive, even if Wolfe is Lyons's brother. Angel's keeping an eye on my apartment while I'm here. My job is held, at least for now. I don't know how long they'll extend my leave without pay, and I don't even know if I want to return to Sutcliffe. I don't think working beside him would be good for me. But I like New York. Nanna was right, it is magical, at least at Christmas. I don't know about the rest of the year."

She looked at the roses again. Wolfe and Angel would've

sent a card. Or did florists just not put cards on flowers to be sent to a cemetery? Did florists even deliver to cemeteries?

"Lord, I have no idea about any of this." Her voice lowered, carried on a sigh. "I should've been here. Mourned for you. Celebrated your life. Something. Not run away."

Once the flowers were arranged, she sat and crossed her legs, and just breathed in silence and felt the early morning sun on her face.

"According to the book I read on the plane about grief, it's okay to sit and say nothing. That way I can hear anything you want to say. Right?"

No response. Not that she'd expected to hear anything. It was a silly woo-woo book, but she'd not found any inspirational, comforting, science-based books on grieving loss. And she'd looked.

It wasn't long before she heard the sound of feet on grass coming from behind her and waited until they were obviously coming closer to her to look.

The sun lit his face, and all the strength seemed to seep out of her body as recognition hit.

Lyons.

Lyons was here. He'd brought the roses.

The realization didn't bring comfort or any lifting of her spirit. It felt like another weight added to already stooped shoulders. She couldn't take care of *him* today. She needed to take care of herself.

What was he even doing there?

She picked herself up from the ground and faced him. He stopped some distance away, close enough for her to talk and look him in the eyes but letting her stay alone inside a bubble around her sister's grave.

In the sunshine, golden undertones appeared in his dark, thick hair, but he looked paler. She'd never seen him in the sunshine; it had been overcast or snowy every day in New York. Probably a trick of the light.

Even if he had decided that he was too hard on her before, the extreme amount of mistrust he had was too much to deal with. Too much to think he looked older because of the way things had ended between them. In truth, standing on her sister's grave, fighting an internal tremor she felt in her chest was the only thing that kept her upright. She was too tired for this, and the only thing she could be thankful for in that moment was that she hadn't yet started crying today. It was still early.

"Why are you here?" she asked directly, not smiling or greeting, or doing anything her normal, welcoming self would do.

"I told you I'd come here with you," he said softly, his eyes searching her face, brows tilted as if seeing her hurt him.

"That was before you decided you hated me."

"I didn't decide that," he answered. "I decided, wrongly, that you had done something awful, exploded and said something more wrong. Unforgivable."

At least he realized that.

She didn't have the strength for this. Not today. The best thing she could do, the only way she could stop the tears burning her eyes, was send him away. If she said anything in response, she'd just prolong the conversation she wasn't up for right now.

"Thank you for the flowers. I don't..." And her control snapped, and a broken sob tore her words in two.

He reached for her, and instinctively she stepped back, until her heels hit the granite. "Can't you see I can't do this?"

He looked pained, guilty, then resigned. She closed her eyes and turned to brace her hands on the top of the tombstone. She couldn't miss the way it mirrored the last time they'd been together, and how much it had hurt when he'd refused *her* touch.

Whether he was going to go, whether he was going to force his presence on her, she didn't know. She couldn't guess, but she wouldn't watch. And she wouldn't let his presence force her to leave.

She folded back to the ground and braced her head on her knees, trying to at least soften the sound of her tears if she couldn't stop them falling.

When she calmed down enough to look, he was gone. He'd listened for once.

"I'm not skipping ahead," she said to her sister, getting her cell again to resume reading, hoping the action calmed her.

"We got through November of last year yesterday.

"That's a year before he enters the picture.

"I'm not skipping ahead. He can wait."

The next day, when she arrived at Noelle's grave, she parked in the place suggested by the direction Lyons had walked in from the day before.

There was a nice car parked there, empty. Looking over the flat land, she could see a man sitting on a bench some distance away, but, even at a distance too great to see his features, she could tell it was Lyons.

She'd not been welcoming, but he'd come back.

As she approached Noelle's grave the man became clearer as well, confirming what her heart had told her. He wasn't close enough to encroach on her or carry on a conversation, but he was there.

He nodded, for some reason, but acknowledging it seemed too much like encouragement for him to approach, so she dropped her chin to the grave. That was when she noticed items waiting. He hadn't brought more flowers today, but a folded-up wool blanket waited for her, along with a little care package—an insulated coffee mug and a wax bag with a pastry inside.

Breakfast, because she came in the morning.

She was tempted to refuse the offerings, but the ground was still damp this morning and sitting on the blanket would be good for her clothes. He was trying to take care of her, but she couldn't even bring herself to tell him he was wasting his time.

She spread out the blanket, sat and tried to ignore him. The daisies were wilting, but the roses still looked nice. She poured more water into the vase, then fished out her phone to call up the emails from April.

"We'll get to him in December," she muttered again, shutting him out and focusing on what she was there for: to get on with life. To learn how to live as half of a pair.

The first day he'd come to the cemetery, he'd brought roses. After she'd told him to go, he'd left. But every day he came back. Not to her—he stayed far enough away so he wasn't pressuring her, just there, if she should want him to be there.

The second day, he'd left a blanket with breakfast. She still didn't want him there.

The third day, he brought fresh flowers, breakfast and a raincoat with a card that said simply: *They call for rain*.

But he wasn't wearing a raincoat. He sat on his bench, overcast sky providing a bleak, gray backdrop behind him.

She never caught him looking at her, and she looked often, but she knew he watched. Waited. There if she needed him.

New Year's Eve, he left a small bottle of champagne and a delicate gold chain looped around the neck of the bottle. A gold, spinning locket, engraved on the back with Noelle's name and date, dangled halfway down the bottle. She got through with eighteen months of email and life summaries and began to speak about him.

It was all right there—the person Nanna and Dad had raised her to be. The beliefs that guided her. And the guilt. She'd been hurt, rightfully, by him, and she'd lashed out. Said something to hurt him back. And she knew it wasn't true. He was there, he'd stayed even though every sign she'd given him had said *go*.

The ball was still in her court. If he was there tomorrow, the fresh start of a new year, maybe she'd talk to him.

She didn't stay up to see the new year or watch the Times Square ball drop on television. She saved the champagne and went to bed to hurry the morning along, then tossed and turned half the night.

New Year's Day she overslept; both the sun and temperatures were higher than normal when she arrived to find workmen installing a gorgeous white wrought-iron bench directly at the foot of Noelle's grave.

Lyons was still at the bench he normally occupied. He was still there.

She'd spent half the night wondering if he would be. Now she had to pluck up the courage to go over to him.

The usual cup of coffee waited for her, with a pastry and some fruit, but no other gifts. Either the bench was his doing, or he was done.

She replayed the gifts she'd given him in her head, trying to think like a man.

Coffee card.

Book.

Strange Scottish fudge stuff.

Scarf set.

She hadn't gotten to see if he'd opened the fancy whiskey she'd purchased because she'd had no idea what to buy for the man whose house she'd never seen, and who probably had two of everything.

As far as giving the same number of gifts as she had, if he had nothing to do with the bench, they were even. He could be at this to even out whatever balance he saw between them. To make a better ending than the one at the massive cabin in the Catskills. Or, maybe he was there to make things right.

The workmen were unhelpful in her attempt to find out if he'd bought the bench, despite working on a national holiday, but while they were there, she wasn't exhibitionist enough to start the daily conversation. Especially as it was all about Lyons since yesterday.

She could sit and watch, or she could go talk to him.

Picking up her breakfast and coffee, she walked toward the bench.

He was instantly alert, and she'd not made it half there, and the look on his face— He didn't even make an attempt to play it cool or aloof. He was *nervous*, but his eyes projected equal parts worry and hope.

Behind him, she could see the same type of bench with a memorial marker as was being placed at Noelle's grave. From him, for sure.

She didn't really have any words, nothing was coming to her, all she could do was look at him to decide what to do or say.

At a distance, she hadn't noticed that his usual polish was gone, but up close she could see he'd gone scruffy, like Wolfe, or like a man who was too worried about other things to deal with a razor.

Despite everything, despite days of her making him wait, of ignoring him, he looked her in the eye, and she could see his sorrow in eyebrows that worried a line on his head, and the way the corners of his mouth actually turned down. Every one of those scruffy beard hairs was a testimony of regret.

"Do you want me to speak first?" he asked, not telling her how this would go. Not telling her anything. Asking.

She asked her own question instead. "You got the bench?"

He nodded, but it was a subdued thing.

"Thank you."

"I don't like you having to sit on the ground."

"Thank you," she said again. "How is it?"

"What?"

"Giving gifts."

His gaze pulled from her face to her throat, and the locket from yesterday, which she wore.

"Nerve-racking," he said after a lengthy pause. "Feels like too little, too late."

She didn't know if it was, she didn't know how this was going to end, so she couldn't offer any words of comfort. She sat on his bench a short distance from where he'd been sitting.

He followed the lead and sat, not touching but closer than if she were a stranger.

"I've been composing my apology in my head since before I got here, but it never works out. In my head, you point out that I was hateful and unappreciative of what I had. I pretty much haven't been able to picture a way to make this work, to say the right thing to make you want to be mine again."

The words, so simply stated, so unguarded, made her eyes prickle again. Different than it had been the past week, not with that deep, terrible burning that started behind her eyes, sizzled down her throat and expanded in her chest to destroy anything good or hopeful she'd had the audacity to foster there. These were hopeful, terrified tears.

"Was I yours?" she asked, her voice frogging up with the effort it took to contain the burning in her eyes. If she looked at him, it'd be all over, she'd bawl again and that would change this conversation. He'd say things to make her stop crying, things that might not be real.

It took him a long time to answer, but when he did, it was a single word. "Yes."

The rasp was his now and jerked her gaze to his face. His eyes were wet.

"You were mine. You weren't just with me, you were part of me." He swallowed a few times, but got it out. "I know it like a man who's lost a limb."

She reached for the locket he'd left her, which she now wore, fisting her hand around the polished gold oval.

He watched her hand, and though he looked momentarily pleased that she'd worn it, his words seemed to register, and he added, hoarsely, "I know it like someone who's lost the most important person in the world, because I did."

Her lower lip quivered, and she had to wipe her eyes again, but the words meant too much—the man who'd lashed out to belittle her sister's existence acknowledging what she'd lost.

"I screwed up, Belle. And I'd do anything for a do-over." He took a breath, slow in and out, then closed his eyes and tilted his face to the sky. "I spent a year wondering what I could've done to prevent Eleni and myself from being shot. Imagining different scenarios, and how would this or that action have changed the outcome for both of us. But I never figured it out."

He opened his eyes then, not hiding anything by looking away. "A week of regret, knowing several things I could've done to change Christmas Eve with you, has eaten through me. Don't say that damned awful thing. Take the time you suggested I take to gather myself. Listen and match what you said with what I knew about you. Any one of those would've changed things."

His fist sat balled on the bench between them, not touching her. Still not touching her. She set her hand down beside his and extended her pinky finger to stroke once over the back of his knuckles.

One touch was all it took. He turned, took her coffee from her and put it on the ground, then pulled her into his lap.

"Please forgive me," he whispered, his hands cupping her cheeks, gaze locked to hers, lashes spiky. "I know I don't deserve you. I know you'd be crazy to take me back, but I'll even take a relationship based on pity credits until I can get into the black."

"What if I told you life with me was a death sentence?" she asked, because, no matter his feelings on it before,

"You're sitting in a cemetery where my whole family is buried."

"Life is a death sentence. However much time I have left, I want to spend with you." He urged her head forward to press a lingering kiss on her forehead, then another at a wet corner of her eye, then down over her salty cheek.

All she could do was nod and his arms came around her, pulling her so that she was cradled to his chest, his scruffy whiskers mashed into her forehead, and tears that weren't hers falling on her cheeks. There were things she wanted to tell him but laying down ground rules seemed unnecessary. They could talk about New York later, make plans, put the promises she felt flowing from him into words.

She had so many holes in her heart, but his arms around her helped, blocked them from leaking out the happiness and contentment that she never seemed to be able to hold on to. Maybe that was what love was between two people who'd lost so much: a promise to continue patching up the holes life put into each other's hearts.

She wasn't ready to let go, would never be ready to let go, but the realization didn't make her feel weak. It made her feel as if she stood in sunshine after a hard, raging storm.

They soaked in the silence for a long time before she said, "I think Christmas will be better next year."

She still felt the shape of the words in her mouth when he answered.

"I know it will."

It was a promise she knew he'd keep.

EPILOGUE

BELLE SAT IN the back seat of the new sedan Lyons had purchased about eight months ago, the day he'd found out he was going to be a daddy. Noelle, their daughter, had very nearly been a Christmas baby. Instead, she'd decided to come into the world twelve days too early, and this trip to the Catskills cabin of last year's fiasco Christmas would be her first Christmas.

The first Christmas for all of them, if Belle thought about it. First Christmas with a happy heart and a whole, healthy family.

"There it is," Lyons said, pulling off the road at the same snail's pace he'd driven there.

She puffed, then shifted again uncomfortably in the seat. Birth hadn't been all that long ago, she hadn't fully recovered yet, but nothing could've kept her away from their Christmas all together. "I thought we'd never make it."

The two-hour drive from Ramapo, where they now lived and worked at Lyons's old hospital, had somehow grown by thirty minutes, with him accounting for the newborn in the back.

He pulled up outside the cabin, and both Wolfe and Angel came hurrying out. Well, Wolfe hurried. Angel, it seemed, had reached the waddling stage a couple of months early.

It took only a moment for them to cover the baby carrier, pass out hugs and kisses, and the lot of them to reach the warm cabin.

"I've sanitized every piece of this place," Angel announced, hand at the small of her back, "She's not gonna be getting anything here. And we've been takin' double doses of vitamin C to make double sure we're not sick before we get to snuggle the Christmas baby."

They all took a moment to pass around Noelle, whose name Lyons had suggested, and which had taken on double the meaning for Belle. Even before she knew how much her daughter would look like the pictures of the two of them as babies. It took her breath at least ten times every day.

"She's not really a Christmas baby," Belle said, sitting down on the plush sofa by the fire, tired despite her excitement.

"She was born a year to the day since we met, and you decided to give me gifts for Christmas," Lyons said, leaning over to kiss her temple. "She's a Christmas baby. Perfectly named."

"Christmas starts in September anyway," Wolfe chimed in, then asked Lyons, "Do you want to get a ride before it gets dark?"

The stables. Scene of the first part of last Christmas's explosion. Belle didn't say anything, just looked up at her husband, who shook his head. "I want to get our bags, and rest with the family. The horses can wait."

The men went to retrieve the luggage, leaving her and Angel in the kitchen, each with a cup of tea Angel had just brewed, and her new sister holding the sleeping newborn and staring down at her, stars in her eyes. The way anyone should look at a baby. Especially a mother. Angel wasn't a mama yet, but in a few months…

"Lyons gave me a gift early," Belle said softly, prompting Angel to look over. "He found my mother. She's alive. Apparently settled down, has a family. He didn't contact her—told me it was up to me. But, I don't know."

Angel's brows shot into her hairline. "He doesn't go half-way on the gifts, does he?"

She laughed a little, and shook her head. "I think we're still trying to figure gifting out."

"Are you going to do it?"

"I don't know," Belle said again, looking at the sleeping baby. It still felt like a betrayal to Noelle, her sister, but for her daughter who was here, and who deserved as big a family as Belle could safely provide her? "I think I will. Lyons said he's vetted them. They're safe."

"If *he's* convinced, pretty sure they're safe. It's up to you."

Belle reached for her cup. "I just hope it works out."

"You hope what works out?" Lyons asked, sitting beside her and taking her hand to give the knuckles a kiss. "And say it quick—you're tired and need to go lay down."

"I hope it works out with Mama. That they're... That they'll be good for us. For Noelle." She swallowed, then added, "I can stay up a little longer, visit awhile. I've been stuck at home for over a week. Noelle's not good at girl-talk yet."

"But she's sleeping, and Wolfe set up a new crib for her in our room. If we want to sleep, might be best to move now," Lyons softly protested.

Wolfe dried his hands from a fresh wash, and sat beside his wife, hands out for the baby. "We can watch her. Uncle's pleasure."

"We do need the practice," Angel added.

"Not that she'll be enough of a workout for us." Wolfe grinned at his wife and then tilted his head toward the two of them.

Lyons looked doubtful and joked, "You haven't seen her diapers."

Relieved of the baby, Angel stepped away to retrieve a little folder from the other room, then waddled back in to place it before them.

Belle opened the file to a sonogram image, but before she could determine what she was looking at, Wolfe said too loudly while holding the baby, "Two. Boys. You wouldn't believe how hard it was to sit on tha' for three months."

Noelle let out a scream at being awakened by a non-daddy male voice, and Lyons went to take her from his brother. "You do seem to need practice speaking at new-dad volume."

It would've sounded like a criticism, except for the way Lyons grabbed his brother by the back of the neck and hauled him against him for a hug once he had his daughter cradled in the other arm. "I'm happy for you. You have the love of a wonderful woman, and you'll both be great parents."

Belle's throat burned, and when she looked at Angel, she could see the dampness in her eyes mirrored there.

This was it. This was the feeling she'd been missing for so long. This was Christmas with family. Even if it was time for the non-traditional Christmas Eve recovering mommy nap.

"We also bought and set up a really pretty wooden rockin' cradle for when we're all downstairs, if she needs to lie down and rest while y'all are sleeping. And we've got everything set up for dinner, ordered ahead, so whenever you're ready we can eat."

"And open presents," Wolfe said, stepping back from his brother's embrace to swipe his eyes.

"I thought we decided on Christmas morning?" Angel said, watching Wolfe as she approached Lyons to reclaim Noelle, now that she'd been calmed with a good, safe Daddy snuggle.

Wolfe made some grumpy sound that basically amounted to, *I'm impatient and I want to do presents.*

She couldn't fault him. The three of them never really had those childhood Christmas wishes fulfilled. If their inner five-year-olds wanted presents tonight, that was fine with her. Belle threw Wolfe a line. "Tomorrow will be pretty full with all the cooking and feasting. Tonight might be better."

He pointed at her, grinning at the backup, and it was settled before Lyons saw her to the room they'd share until after New Year's.

Just as they settled in on the comfy bed, his arms around her, nose in her hair, he sang in a whisper in her ear, "Do you hear what I hear?"

She chuckled, shaking her head. "No?"

"Silence. I suspect we'll have an hour before one of us has to go settle her down when Wolfe gets too loud again."

"Shh. I only have an hour to sleep before you get up to go settle Noelle down."

He quieted, but before either of them drifted off, she whispered, "Merry Christmas, my love."

"Christmas will be better next year." He said to her the words she'd said at her sister's grave and gave a gentle squeeze.

Again, her throat thickened, and she closed her eyes, squeezing his arm draped over her.

No matter how perfect this Christmas already seemed, every day with him was a gift, better than the day before, and next year they'd have a one-year-old to rip open presents.

His words last year were the only ones that fit, and she whispered them back. "I know it will."

* * * * *

COMING SOON!

We really hope you enjoyed reading this book. If you're looking for more romance, be sure to head to the shops when new books are available on

Thursday 27th December

To see which titles are coming soon, please visit
millsandboon.co.uk

MILLS & BOON

Coming next month

TEMPTED BY HER SINGLE DAD BOSS
Annie O'Neil

Their heads touched, lightly. They both looked up and at each other. He could feel her breath on his lips. He wanted to cup her face in his hands and kiss her. And not just any old kiss. An urgent, hungry, satiating kiss. Something that would answer all of the questions he'd had from the moment he'd laid eyes on her. Something that would tell him if all of this was a hallucination or very, very real.

'Ready, Doc?'

He nodded, not entirely sure what he was saying he was ready for.

Maggie sat back in the chair and detached her prosthetic, their eyes still locked on each other's. He was going to kiss her. Resistance seemed…ridiculous. Why wait for something he'd never known he wanted?

So he did.

He didn't hover nervously. Offer tentative butterfly kisses. No. His mouth crashed down on hers as if he'd been waiting for this moment his entire life.

From the moment his mouth touched hers, he knew that lightning could strike twice. That there was more than one woman he'd been meant to kiss. To hold. To cup her face between his hands. To taste as the water poured over the pair of them, erasing time, history, anything and everything that up until this moment would've kept them apart.

It wasn't a one-sided kiss. Not by a long shot. Maggie's entire body was arching up and toward him. She'd woven her fingers through his hair and was sliding her other hand along his stubble as their kisses gained in intensity.

Just as he was about to slip his hands onto her waist and pull her even closer to him, the bathroom door abruptly slammed open.

Alex pulled himself away from Maggie and turned just in time to see his son walk through the door.

Jake. His little boy. A mop of sandy blond hair, just like his. Brown eyes like his mother's. As if he'd ever forget who had brought this child into the world. His serious, intense, loving son who'd gone through all but a single year of his life without his mother.

'Hey, Dad.' Jakes eyebrows tugged together as he took in the scene then noticed that Maggie was holding one of her legs in her hand. His eyes widened further than Alex had ever seen them.

'Oh....' His eyebrows rose up to his hairline. 'Cool....'

Continue reading
TEMPTED BY HER SINGLE DAD BOSS
Annie O'Neil

Available next month
www.millsandboon.co.uk

LET'S TALK
Romance

For exclusive extracts, competitions
and special offers, find us online:

f facebook.com/millsandboon

🐦 @MillsandBoon

📷 @MillsandBoonUK

Get in touch on 01413 063232

For all the latest titles coming soon, visit
millsandboon.co.uk/nextmonth